# Robin Hood

## by Larry Blamire

Baker's Plays
P.O. Box 699222
Quincy, MA 02269-9222

*Western States Representative*
Samuel French, Inc.
7623 Sunset Blvd.
Hollywood CA 90046

*Canadian Representative*
Samuel French, Ltd.
100 Lombard St., Lower Level
Toronto, M5C 1M3 Canada

# NOTICE

ROBIN HOOD

*Robin Hood* was presented by the Open Door Theatre of Boston, directed by Michael Poisson with the aid of the following crew:

*Sets by* Perry Barton
*Lights by* Brooke Stark
*Costume Design by* Michael Homisak
*Fight Choreography by* Henry Woronicz

Producers...............Perry Barton, Patrick English,
Jean Klugman, Susan McGinley
Stage Manager........................ Richard Callahan
Assistant Stage Manager....................Billy Donald
Technical Director .............. Matthew Bagedonow
Light Board ............................ Nancy LaFarge
Publicity ...............................Susan McGinley
Photography ................................ Tom Bloom
Layout ...................................... Perry Barton
Graphics....................................Larry Blamire
Costume, Set and Prop Crews...Cast of Robin Hood
and members of ODT

# CAST
## (In order of appearance)

Will Gamwell (later Scarlet)..........Kevin Colarusso
Robin Hood...............................Larry Blamire
Marian Harper .................................. Marina Re
Riccon Hazel..................... Matthew Bagedonow
The Sheriff of Nottingham..........Clifford M. Allen
The Bishop of Hereford..............Mike McNamara
William, the Sheriff's steward.............Mark Solari
King John .................................... David Baird
Little John ............................... Sidney Atwood
Much.............................................Ed White
Arthur-a-Bland.............................Frank Dixon
Scathelock....................................R. Randall
Alan-a-Dale............................ Carl John Nolan
Ellen Deirwold.............................Brooke Stark
Eadom ................................. Richard Callahan
Catherine ..........................Susan B. McConnell
Meg ............................................. Karen Kelly
Queen Eleanor of Aquitane........... Nola Bonecutter
Friar Tuck ................................. Paul Stickney
The Prioress of Kirklees...............Wendy Almeida
Guy of Gisbourne................Thomas J. Vittorioso
Foresters..................Billy Donald, Jeff L. Schake
                                             Andrew Papagikos

# CHARACTERS

Will Gamwell (later Scarlet)
Robin Hood
Marian Harper
Riccon Hazel
The Sheriff of Nottingham
The Bishop of Hereford
Hilton, the Sheriff's female attendant
King John
Little John
Much
Arthur-a-Bland
Meg Scathelocke
Alan-a-Dale
Ellen Deirwold
Eadom
Catherine
Queen Eleanor of Aquitane
Friar Tuck
The Prioress of Kirklees
Guy of Gisbourne
Various of the King's Foresters, Musicians, and
    Common Folk

## SCENE

In and around Sherwood Forest, Nottingham and London, England.

## TIME

The Middle Ages.

## ACT I

### Scene 1

*SETTING: Sherwood Forest; A lush green wood with an open clearing and various trails of access, dominated by a particularly large oak tree.*

*AT RISE: It is early morning. The forest is silent for a moment, but is soon rudely broken by the raucous singing of a drunken WILL GAMWELL, somewhere off.*

WILL. *(Off.)* Ohhhhh metaphysical tobaccoooo!! ... Fetched ... as far off from Moroccoooo!! ...

*(ROBIN HOOD and WILL GAMWELL enter from one of the paths. They are both woodsmen scruffily dressed in greens and browns and armed with bows and arrows. WILL is also armed with a wine sack, and he's not afraid to use it.)*

WILL. Ohhhhh metaphysical tobaccoooo!!...

ROBIN. You know, you make it difficult to hunt buck with all that caterwauling. The only deer left in Sherwood are the ones that are deaf.

WILL. But, I'm just trying to confuse them, Robin. They'll think we're traveling minstrels. And when they all gather in a circle to hear my sweet song. Zoom! Off go the arrows—on come the plates of venison.

7

ROBIN. Will, I can't deny it, it's a wonderful idea. And to make it better, what say we spread out some chairs and cushions, a table full of fruit, set up a ticket stand.

WILL. (*Staring at him.*) You're making fun of me ... You're making fun of me, aren't you ... *I* come up with the ideas ... and *you* make fun of me.

ROBIN. Yes, and it's an excellent idea—assuming the King's deer could be as as stupid as he is.

WILL. Mmmm I see what you mean. Not likely.

ROBIN. No.

WILL. Bloody stupid King John—Ya know if Richard the Lion-Hearted hadn't died—

ROBIN. I know, bloody inconsiderate, wasn't it?

WILL. Absolutely ! Absolutely ! (*Starting to drink again.*)

ROBIN. Come on, Will, not on an empty stomach. Look what happens to you.

WILL. Well, feed me some venison then, if you're so bothered.

(*A NOISE of movement comes from the forest. ROBIN and WILL freeze and listen a moment. ROBIN speaks quietly.*)

ROBIN. I think I'll do just that.

(*HE slaps WILL on the arm and the two of them scurry off to one side, hiding in the brush. MARIAN HARPER enters from a path. She is extremely attractive despite a rather woodsy attire of cap and buckskin. SHE stalks quietly for deer with a shaft ready in her bow.*)

ROBIN. Who is she? Do you know her?

WILL. Just another poor Saxon looking for breakfast.

ROBIN. Aye, she's different though. Think I 'd like to meet her.

WILL. Oh no. Not "The Rescue."

ROBIN. "The Rescue." I should appear in the best possible light, don't you think?

*(ROBIN slaps him on the back, then heads into the woods to circle around behind. WILL waits as MARIAN approaches. Then HE draws his sword and leaps into the clearing with the great flourish and roaring voice of a villain from a melodrama.)*

WILL. Ah-haaa!! A beautiful maiden!! And she's alone!! What *luck*!! Satan must be smiling today!! How fortunate for me!! How unfortunate for you!! You will rue the day you met up with ... *the Baron Hardankles*!!

MARIAN. *(Wary but cool.)* What if I don't feel like ruing?

*(Unfazed by this, WILL strikes a fearsome pose.)*

WILL. Yaaahhhh!!

MARIAN. What are you doing?

WILL. *(Different pose.)* Ya-haaa!!

MARIAN. Would you mind telling me what you're doing?

WILL. *(Dropping the character a moment.)* What? *(Back into his Hardankles pose.)* Well!! I'll tell you what I'm doing, if you so want to know so much!! Now will I, the Baron Hardankles, pluck me forth a fresh flower of Saxon maidenhead—*hood*!! Say your prayers!! For who will save you now?!

MARIAN. Go ahead and try. I'm waiting.

WILL. (*Dropping character, blankly.*) You're waiting? Waiting for what?

MARIAN. Go ahead and pluck, if you're going to pluck.

WILL. (*Quietly confused.*) Yes, but you really should resist—

ROBIN. (*Leaps valiantly into the scene from the other direction, with an equal amount of ham.*) Hold, oh thou Norman piglet!! Ravish not this fair maiden!! For I have three feet of cold steel shall make a sieve of thee!!

MARIAN. Let him come, it's fine.

ROBIN. (*Quickly.*) No, it's no trouble really—

WILL. Saxon dog!! Who art thou, that thou wouldst cross me in battle so?!

ROBIN. *Vile chicken-headed thing*!! My name shalt be thy last knowledge in life!! I am he whom men call ... *Robin Hood*!!

WILL. (*Covering face.*) Gaaahh!!...

ROBIN. Yes cringe! And pray now to whatever deity watches over the swine of Norman knighthood—*If any*!! Take that! And that!

(*WILL defends as ROBIN applies broad strokes of the sword— none capable of the slightest damage. MARIAN watches with a rather wry look on her face.*)

ROBIN. Thou loathesome hound of hell!!

(*WILL screams as ROBIN applies the death blow on the side farthest from Marian. WILL crumples to the ground.*)

WILL. Oh. I am slain ...

ROBIN. It is done.

WILL. Live no longer ...
ROBIN. It is finished.
WILL. I die—
ROBIN. You're dead—Yes!

*(WILL cuts short the scene and dies. ROBIN turns to Marian.)*

ROBIN. He'll trouble you no more, fair Saxon maid.

MARIAN. He didn't trouble me at all—Didn't even touch me. All he did was yell a lot.

ROBIN. Yes, frightening. Once again I'm forced to take a life—Yea, a wretched, depraved, meaningless Norman life—but ... a life, nonetheless.

MARIAN. There's no blood on your sword.

ROBIN. What?

MARIAN. There's no blood on your sword. It's clean.

ROBIN. *(Quickly looks at the sword. Slowly, as if personally offended.)* Why the bloodless wretch ... *(To Marian.)* Typical Norman, wouldn't you know? Thinner than water. *(Quickly sheathing the sword.)*

MARIAN. Well, I think I've had enough entertainment for one day. Thank you, good Riding Hood.

ROBIN. Robin.

MARIAN. Riding Robin, yes. Good day.

ROBIN. Well, I can hardly let you go unescorted. I didn't save that pretty neck to have it slit as soon as you enter the wood.

*(MARIAN starts walking. ROBIN tags along after her.)*

MARIAN. Oh, but I've been so looking forward to that. Now how am I to have my pretty neck slit if you keep tagging after me? Or my eyes put out—

ROBIN. Lovely eyes—

MARIAN. Or my head chopped off—

ROBIN. A magnificent head—

MARIAN. (*Turns, drawing her sword in a single smooth move, pointing it at Robins's chest.*) It should be. *It's the head of a Norman.*

(*MARIAN slowly backs the startled ROBIN up.*)

MARIAN. A wretched, depraved, meaningless Norman ...Which is what I happen to be.

(*For once ROBIN is at a loss for words. HE stands dumbly with his mouth open. Suddenly four of the KING'S FORESTERS, the soldiers for the area, enter from the woods. Their chief is RICCON HAZEL. They are all rough low-lifes in uniform.*)

RICCON. Hold right there!

(*RICCON stands over the body of Will as the OTHER THREE spread out in a half-circle.*)

RICCON. Well well well ... I don't know which one a' ya murdered him, but ya both gonna come along with me. The Sheriff'll decide.

MARIAN. Now see here, I'm not going anywhere. Do you know who I am? I'm Marian Harper, chief lady-in-waiting to Her Majesty Queen Eleanor herself.

*(ROBIN looks at her sharply. The FORESTERS are amused.)*

RICCON. Ohhh yesss ... Pardon us, Marian, we didn't recognize you there. Well look. You'll be happy to see we've brought Queen Eleanor with us. Say hello, Eleanor.

1ST FORESTER. Hello.

2ND FORESTER. And I'm lovely Helen of Troy. We must all get together for tea later on.

*(The FORESTERS snicker contemptuously.)*

RICCON. Why wait? Let's go have some now. Come along.

*(MARIAN levels her sword at them. THEY halt.)*

MARIAN. I warn you. You're making a dangerous mistake.

*(RICCON and the FORESTERS draw their swords.)*

RICCON. I arrest you in the name of the Lord High Sheriff of Nottingham and Nottinghamshire in whose woods you now trespass—

ROBIN. *(Who had been stunned up to this point by Marian's revelation, finally shakes his head.)* Look, this has gone far enough. Will? Will, get up. The joke's over ...Will?

*(WILL remains motionless. The FORESTERS look at Riccon and then begin to close in, stepping over Will's body.)*

ROBIN. (*A weak chuckle.*) It was just a joke—*Will*?!
Show the Royal Foresters you're alive now so they won't kill
us, all right? Look, this is ridiculous. That's my friend Will
Gamwell. We were just out hunting deer when—

(*RICCON and the FORESTERS react with broad "Ohhhs" and
"Ah-ha's".*)

MARIAN. That was bright.
RICCON. Hunting the King's deer! Well, we won't bring
you in after all.
ROBIN. You won't?
RICCON. No no. We'll hang ya right here.
MARIAN. I have special permission to hunt the King's
deer.
RICCON. You have special permission to sprout wings
and fly away.
ROBIN. I see. We're supposed to go hungry, is that it?
Well if I can't fill my belly—(*Quickly drawing his sword.*) I'll
just have to fill yours instead!

(*The FORESTERS halt at this. THEY are in a half-circle
around Robin and Marian with their backs to Will.*)

ROBIN. Well, who's going to be first, my fat little friends?
I haven't got all day!

(*The FORESTERS look uncertainly at each other.*)

1ST FORESTER. Who *is* gonna be first?
RICCON. (*An angry bark.*) None of us is who, you twit!
We all rush together!

*(WILL rises from the ground behind them, sword ready.)*

ROBIN. It's about time you rejoined the living.
2ND FORESTER. Don't even try it, Bucko.
WILL. Sorry, Robin. Hadda sleep off a hangover.

*(The FORESTERS turn, startled.)*

ROBIN. How d'ya feel now?
WILL. Rested and ready to go.
ROBIN. Good! Time to carve up the King's fat juicy venison!

*(ROBIN strikes and a battle ensues. With obvious skill, HE and MARIAN take on RICCON and the 1ST and 2ND FORESTERS while WILL takes on the 3RD. After some furious clashing, MARIAN wounds the 1ST and HE scurries off. The 3RD falls to the ground and WILL wounds him. ROBIN battles RICCON on one side and the 2ND FORESTER on the other. RICCON sees they are now outnumbered.)*

RICCON. Come on!

*(HE and the 2ND FORESTER go to the aid of the wounded 3RD and help him off. WILL goes over to ROBIN and the two of them laugh after the fleeing enemy. MARIAN collects her bow and quiver.)*

MARIAN. I suggest you two take time out from laughing to go hide somewhere. The Sheriff of Nottingham has a wicked reputation.

ROBIN. I'm sure *Her Ladyship* must have heard that in the *court* sometime.

MARIAN. That's my advice. Take it or leave it, Saxon.

WILL. (*Laughing.*) What about you? You weren't exactly *dancing* with your man.

MARIAN. (*Smiling.*) Fortunately, they didn't believe I'm who I am. In which case ... the only name they have ... is yours, *Will Gamwell.*

(*Smugly SHE heads off into the woods. WILL and ROBIN look at each other, no longer so amused. BLACKOUT.*)

**End of Scene 1**

**ACT I**

**Scene 2**

*SETTING: The open terrace of the great hall of Nottingham Castle. Surrounded by a low stone railing, this is the area where the Sheriff receives guests, prisoners, and anyone else. He conducts his business there around a large banquet table—excellent for storming about in a huff as he often does. There are also stools to kick over and a large divan. Torches and banners offer limited decoration. Behind all this is the door leading to the great hall and the castle beyond.*

*AT RISE: It is later in the same day. The SHERIFF, lean and hawk-like in dark clothing, paces in a restless mood. His ubiquitous guest, THE BISHOP OF HEREFORD, lies on the divan as always, eating noisily from a bowl of fruit. He is quite corpulent and over-jewelled. His manner is effete, his enunciation—too, too perfect. HILTON, the SHERIFF'S unctuous female attendant, stands on duty in the doorway.*

SHERIFF. What is wrong with this terrace? Why doesn't it look right? Here I have King John coming and the most important part of the castle—The place where I receive, entertain, transact, destroy—just doesn't look right to me! No matter what I do! Maybe it's too austere—some more tapestries—But I don't want it to look cluttered. Is something out of place? I just can't put my finger on it!

BISHOP. You are much too much too worrisome, my Lord Sheriff. I do swear I can see raw nerve endings jutting from your temples like tiny pennants waving in the wind. I've seen this before. Your face will turn bright plum, the tendons bunching up like a pack of dogs wrestling for meat, while the veins in your throat start rippling like some loathsome congregation of worms. In Hereford we have a saying, "The only thing hotter than the heat, is the fire."

SHERIFF. *(Stops pacing and stares at him a moment.)* And from whom did you glean that pearl of wisdom, my Lord Bishop?

BISHOP. Well of course, that's not actually a saying, in that no one actually said that, although I'm sure I heard it somewhere—In fact, I might have even said it myself—The point I'm trying to make is, things could always be worse.

Therefore, we must continue to remain calm, like me, through all manner of storms, floods, volcanic interruptions—

*(The SHERIFF resumes pacing.)*

BISHOP. ... and visits from King John; all of which come under the heading: Great Forces of Nature. Do not shrink from greatness, but rise up to meet it—

SHERIFF. What is wrong with this room?

BISHOP. ... Grasp it by the royal antlers, so to speak, look him squarely in the eye, and proclaim—

SHERIFF. *(Turning on him suddenly.)* It is you!! It is you that is wrong with this room!! That's it!! That's it!! Oh, I am content now!!

BISHOP. *(Calmly.)* You see? There they go. Those horrible veins.

SHERIFF. Shut up!! Shut up, Hereford!! Finally I have found the source of this disorder!!

BISHOP. Like throbbing blue caterpillars—

SHERIFF. Everything else in here is quite pleasing!! The decor is positively scrupulous!! But you!! You're always there, spewing words like noxious gas, like some sort of lazy lunatic grandmother!!

BISHOP. Oh, now the blood's boiling, swelling your head, until like an overripe melon, it can do naught but explode. Then you'll really have to worry about the appearance of the room, unless King John is taken with the idea of Sheriff's brains as decorative regalia—a thought I find as amusing as it is revolting.

SHERIFF. And put that fruit down!! Slurping it into that great mouth one after another like some obscene denizen of the ocean's bottom!!

BISHOP. Well, don't put them out then.

*(KING JOHN enters behind them in the doorway. He is a small, soft-spoken, fastidious tyrant who always seems both amused and superior.)*

HILTON. My Lord, the Ki—
SHERIFF. Not now, Hilton!!
KING. Did the fruit go bad?
SHERIFF. Stuff the fruit—!!... *(HE spins and abruptly freezes at the sight of King John. HE hastily bows.)* My liege.
BISHOP. *(Nodding.)* Your Majesty.
KING. *(Strolling casually about the room.)* Rise, rise, my Lord Sheriff. Rise ... to wealth, to fame ... to *your own barony. (Pause.)* But first ... rise to patience. Rise to tolerance and understanding—It is therein that greatness lies. Can we defeat an enemy we don't understand? I think not. No more than we can gain the respect and loyalty of valuable friends through hostile bullying and infantile rages. *(Briefly shakes the Bishop's hand then sits in a chair, examining the fruit without eating.)* If you plant fear in people you only fuel their instinct for self-preservation and, believe you me, there is no disease more dangerous among the servile. They are so, so impressionable; soldiers, cooks, bookkeepers—pieces of clay waiting for the right hands. But they must be sensitive hands or the art becomes malformed. Given proper care, however, they will gladly die for you. With complete trust in their master, he need but bid them enter the hideous jaws of death and they will march proudly and unflagging to their doom and ... to their respective hereafters.
SHERIFF. If His Majesty thinks for a moment I'm going to mollycoddle the monkeys and buffoons I'm supplied with he

is sadly mistaken. I find it difficult enough not bludgeoning My Lord Bishop never mind the bloody cook.

KING. You will be quite civil to My Lord Bishop. Herefordshire is an important part of my power. Now I realize that a complete transformation of one's innate temperament doesn't happen overnight. You have one week. Now, to more important matters.

BISHOP. Are there any?

*(The KING and BISHOP have a polite laugh over this, much to the annoyance of the SHERIFF.)*

KING. Oh dear ...Well we certainly know there *are* more serious matters. For instance in the area of tax collection. We seem to be meeting a little resistance here, are we not?

SHERIFF. Why, there's not a county in the realm—

KING. No, we are not meeting a little resistance, we are meeting a *lot* of resistance.

SHERIFF. Since the last increase, tax collection has become the single greatest expenditure in the Kingdom—

KING. You're telling *me* that? You're telling *me* that? You're barely breaking even—You're telling *me* that?

SHERIFF. I'm telling you because you don't seem to be aware of the cost and difficulty involved—

KING. Nottinghamshire is breaking records in tax resistance, is it not?

SHERIFF. I haven't charted the rest of the Kingdom! I have more important things to do!

KING. *Nothing*! *Nothing* is more important to me than income! *(Calming from this brief outburst.)* Four years ago when my brother the Lion-Hearted had the good sense to die, he also had the good sense to place the crown on my head.

Unfortunately he neglected to give me the majesty that goes with it ... I look in the mirror and I see a crown, but do I see a king? No. At least not while my mother lives. Eleanor has not only more power and glamour, she also holds sway over the barons. Without money, and without the support of the barons I cannot execute my fondest dream; The invasion of my former ally, Philip of France. Only then will the true King of England stare back at me from the mirror. My mother, I'll deal with later ... The taxes ... we'll deal with now, *my Lord Sheriff* ...

SHERIFF. You know what Nottinghamshire's like. We have much more than our share of troublemakers and vagrants.

BISHOP. Oh, I don't know, they seem to be everywhere. Like insects. I swear I can hardly ride the streets without being forced to gaze upon disagreeable faces. And me a man of God! Do they bow to me? No! There's all these raised heads. I think the only time they lower their heads is when they're sucking on a horse trough. In fact, my *horse* shows me more reverence! I had a man whipped yesterday for cursing in my presence— cursing, mind you! He dropped something on his foot—an axe or something—and set forth with a litany of such foul vulgarity—

SHERIFF. Hereford—

BISHOP. That it was enough to make even my Lord Sheriff blush, I do say—

SHERIFF. Bishop!!

KING. I'm sure you have your rabble too, Hereford, however, nowhere do they thrive with such robust abandon as they do under my Lord Sheriff's nose.

SHERIFF. I have just instituted harsher penalties—

KING. Let me see your books.

*(Pause.)*

SHERIFF. I have barely instituted these measures. You can hardly expect them to show an effect, already. Am I to magically transform the temperament of an entire county along with my own? Perhaps I could offer a prize—A new horse if you pay your taxes on time. How about a tour of the Bishop's castle? A good look at that bejewelled lump over there—that'll inspire them.

*(Pause. The KING studies him coolly.)*

KING. (*Slowly, quietly.*) Talk he to me thus ... (*Suddenly lightening up again.*) And yet ... *He lives.* The man begs to be put to death—Here's my head, he says. But *such* is *my* patience ... *my* understanding ... that here the man stands— (*Close to the Sheriff, quiet again.*) ... knowing he trod close to the river of death ... and found the gentle bridge I layed out for him. The rest of your life, Sheriff ... shall be your lesson. And my gift.

*(Pause. The SHERIFF realizes how close he came.)*

SHERIFF. (*Screaming.*) Hilton!!
HILTON. Aye, Good My Lord.
SHERIFF. Fetch the books.

*(HILTON exits.)*

SHERIFF. I have given permission for the Royal Foresters to perform on the spot executions, provided I get the heads—

KING. Take the heads, keep the heads, make them into flower pots if you like—I want their money.

HILTON. (*Enters with ledger books.*) My Lord, Riccon Hazel is here to see you. He says it's urgent.

SHERIFF. Not now! Can't you see we're—!

KING. Oh, that's all right. It'll give me a chance to peruse them.

*(HE takes the books from HILTON who goes to the door and gestures for RICCON who enters immediately.)*

RICCON. M'Lord.

SHERIFF. Ah, my dear Riccon.

RICCON. (*Halts abruptly.*) Are you ... feeling all right, M'Lord?

SHERIFF. Of course I'm all right! What—what's your business?

RICCON. It's not good. One of the Foresters is dead, M'Lord.

SHERIFF. Dead? How?

RICCON. Well, these two men and a woman, see? They were playin' this game. And one of 'em wasn't *really* dead. See, but—

SHERIFF. What?!

RICCON. Oh ...Well, I mean they was huntin' King's deer. We tried to arrest them and they got away. One Forester died from his wounds.

SHERIFF. Who were they? I want names.

RICCON. One of 'em's called Will Gamwell. He's the one who did our man. The woman—huh! She was a real corker. Tried ta tell us she was Marian Harper, lady to Queen Eleanor.

*(The KING looks up from the books with great interest.)*

SHERIFF. *(Disdainfully.)* Queen Eleanor—How could you let these—Never mind. I'll issue a warrant for Will Gamwell. Find out who the others are.

RICCON. I'm told this Gamwell frequents the Blue Boar Inn at Lincoln.

SHERIFF. Blue Boar Inn. That strikes a bell. *(HE goes through one of the ledgers.)* Oh yes. Blue Boar. Extremely obstinate in their collections. *(HE closes it and ponders quietly.)* Perhaps a visit to Lincoln is in order.

*(Without looking HE waves RICCON to exit and HE does. The KING steps up beside the SHERIFF who's deep in thought.)*

KING. Make me a wealthy man ... and I'll make you ... a baron.

*(The SHERIFF slowly smiles as HE turns to look at the KING who also smiles. BLACKOUT.)*

## End of Scene 2

## ACT I

### Scene 3

*AT RISE: The following day in Sherwood Forest. ROBIN HOOD enters and approaches a log or small bridge. This might span a ditch or a suggested stream—depending on the ingenuity of the production. ROBIN is about to cross when a large, grim, bearded man carrying a quarterstaff—LITTLE JOHN—enters from the other side, barring the way.*

ROBIN. Hup! Hold on. You there, good fellow. Why don't you hold a second there and let me cross before you mount the log, there's a good lad.

*(ROBIN takes a step onto the log and LITTLE JOHN takes one also.)*

ROBIN. Hup hup hup! Excuse me! Good gentleman! Do you see what you're doing? Look what you're doing. See, that's not quite what I had in mind. If you start your great bulk across, then I'll be forced to wait here on the other side and play witness to your lumbering progress. Now ordinarily, I'd be only too happy to sit here and take a nap while you waddle along, but as it is, I'm heading to the Blue Boar Inn hoping to find a certain lady there. You know what they say about a lady-in-waiting—They *don't.*

*(ROBIN laughs a bit forced at this lame jest, but this turns into a throat-clearing when the grim LITTLE JOHN fails to react.)*

ROBIN. Yes, well, if you don't mind—

*(HE takes a step. LITTLE JOHN does also.)*

LITTLE JOHN. Ugh!

ROBIN. (*Halting again.*) A man of few words. Are you a man of action? Then go away. Go.

(*LITTLE JOHN doesn't move.*)

ROBIN. Oh, I get it! Perhaps you're a poor dumb fellow! Can you speak? (*As to a child.*) Speak ... Speak ... Come on, little fella' ... Hm. Are you deaf too? Is that it? Ah, ya poor, poor brute. Well, this is your lucky day, for Robin Hood has taken pity on you. And I'm digging deep in my pocket to come up with—(*Pulls a coin out of his pocket.*) Tuppence! Ooooooo—Tuppence! Ahhhhhh! (*ROBIN tosses it across to the other side.*) Get the coin. Fetch the coin, little fella', ya bloody stupid oaf.

LITTLE JOHN. (*Slowly, grimly.*) I'm not deaf ... I'm not dumb ... I won't go ... And—(*HE spits.*) ... I spit on your tuppence.

(*Pause.*)

ROBIN. I see, oh thou mighty oaf—oak, I meant to say. Well, this is a problem, isn't it. You won't back off the log?

LITTLE JOHN. Mm!

ROBIN. Was that a yes or a no?

LITTLE JOHN. I'd much rather you step aside, little man. I've had more than enough sport for one day.

ROBIN. How 'bout a little archery?

(*ROBIN fixes a shaft in his bow. LITTLE JOHN studies this action calmly.*)

LITTLE JOHN. What are you going to do? Shoot me with your bow and arrow?

ROBIN. (*Looking at his bow a moment.*) Well, yes, I s'pose I'll have to.

LITTLE JOHN. (*A deep gravelly chuckle.*) Now, isn't that right sporting of ya. Shoot a man with a bow and arrow who's armed only with a quarterstaff. (*A grim laugh.*)

ROBIN. A what? Oh, ya mean your stick. Is that what that is?

LITTLE JOHN. Yes. Feel it with your head.

ROBIN. (*Chuckling.*) No no, that's all right, thank you.

LITTLE JOHN. Go ahead, I insist.

ROBIN. (*Still chuckling, nodding his head.*) All right. All right, my poor addled friend. I suppose I can't just shoot you. Never let it be said Robin Hood's not a fair man. Wait here a moment.

(*LITTLE JOHN waits calmly while ROBIN rushes into the wood. We hear him humming a tune while HE thrashes about in the brush.*)

LITTLE JOHN. Should I sit down for a while?

ROBIN. (*Off.*) Coming, slow witted dull thing! (*HE rushes back in with a crudely fashioned quarterstaff of his own.*) There! Now we can—Hold on a moment here ... Did you take a step forward?

LITTLE JOHN. I did not move an inch.

ROBIN. (*Patronizingly.*) C'mon, you little elf, tell the truth now. You did move forward just a little, didn't you.

LITTLE JOHN. (*Slow burn.*) Call you me a liar, you?

ROBIN. *Call you me a liar, you* ... If you attack me, the way you attack the King's English, I'd better be on my toes.

LITTLE JOHN. I mighta' known you'd speak the *King's* English, you bloody Norman.

ROBIN. (*Finally rankled.*) Norman!... I've been patient with you, fellow. Prepare yourself for a sound drubbing. Your stomach will make a fine laundry bag!

(*ROBIN swipes quickly three times with his staff. The practiced LITTLE JOHN easily blocks the attacks, seemingly without effort. ROBIN ends the quick series with a complete spin and a mighty swipe. LITTLE JOHN casually moves his stick and ROBIN misses entirely, spinning all the way around. HE stands rather blankly, not quite sure what happened. THEY resume, this time LITTLE JOHN taking a more active part. Soon HE has the better of ROBIN who receives more than his share of whacks. THEY lock, straining in a coeur-de-coeur. ROBIN is losing.*)

LITTLE JOHN. Don't worry, lad. I'll see your mother gets both your ears.

ROBIN. (*Reacts strongly, eyes going wide.*) My mother!... My mother's dead ...

(*LITTLE JOHN eases off the staff.*)

ROBIN. She died last week ...

(*THEY lower their staffs. ROBIN lowers his head in sorrow.*)

LITTLE JOHN. I'm sorry, fellow. I did not know.

*(As LITTLE JOHN lowers his head, ROBIN suddenly jams the staff into Little John's foot. HE cries out, hopping up and down. ROBIN quickly thwacks him twice, sending him stumbling backwards.)*

ROBIN. You are a *thick* block a' wood, aren't ya.

*(With a mighty roar LITTLE JOHN raises his staff and charges. ROBIN defends the assault with vigor, enjoying the contest. However, he soon finds getting LITTLE JOHN angry was a costly mistake, as the larger man starts to beat him down.)*

ROBIN. I suppose ... you're ... a fair enough ... opponent—

*(A mighty blow disarms ROBIN who flails, reaching over for his staff. LITTLE JOHN casually taps his rear with his staff and ROBIN, arms wheeling, tumbles from the log. ROBIN lands and sits, stunned, looking about. LITTLE JOHN roars a laugh and ROBIN snickers, shaking his head.)*

ROBIN. Oh, so *that's* a quarterstaff.
LITTLE JOHN. I must admit you took your drubbing like a man.
ROBIN. Well, give me a hand then.

*(LITTLE JOHN reaches down. ROBIN takes his hand and suddenly tries to yank. LITTLE JOHN, solid as a mountain, gives a wry smile. ROBIN chuckles haplessly*

*and allows himself to be hauled up. WILL enters the same
way Robin came in.)*

WILL. Had a fall, did ya?
ROBIN. Yes, I had a— ... Well, thrashing's more like it, if
you must know.
WILL. Heading to the Blue Boar?
ROBIN. Aye. Say, why don't you join us, friend, and let
me buy you an ale?
LITTLE JOHN. No man buys an ale for John Little of
Mansfield.

*(WILL laughs. LITTLE JOHN looks grim.)*

LITTLE JOHN.  What's funny? *Mansfield*?
WILL. No, *Little*.

*(LITTLE JOHN starts to nod then considers this possible
    insult. ROBIN steps in.)*

ROBIN. I'm Robin Hood of Locksley. This is my friend
Will—
WILL. ... Scarlet. Will Scarlet's the name.

*(ROBIN looks at him, remembering the reason for his name
    change.)*

LITTLE JOHN. Mm. Well, I suppose all this unnecessary
gabbin' has worked me up a proper thirst.
ROBIN. Good! Let's off then.

*(THEY start to head off. WILL chuckles quietly to himself.)*

WILL. Little John ...

*(HE chuckles again and LITTLE JOHN fixes him with a glare as THEY exit. BLACKOUT.)*

**End of Scene 3**

**ACT I**

**Scene 4**

*SETTING: For the rustic setting of the Blue Boar Inn, Sherwood Forest can be used quite nicely. A long table, some benches, a board across two barrels for the bar, a few kegs and the inn is complete.*

*AT RISE: Minutes have lapsed. We find the inn in its usual spirit of good cheer with laughter, drinking and dancing. ALAN-A-DALE, a young minstrel, provides the music on a lute, while beautiful young ELLEN DEIRWOLD, his fiancée, dances. CATHERINE, the hostess of the inn, dances with ARTHUR-A-BLAND, the local tanner, while her husband, EADOM, frantically fills the ales. MEG SCATHELOCKE, a rough cockney-speaking woman, dances also, while MUCH the miller, always addled but with great flourish, hops around. ALAN ends the song amid clapping and cheers.*

MUCH. A well-dressed song, Alan-a-Dale! Brilliantly danced! You have feet like ancient crabs!

ARTHUR. Keep drinking, Much! You're starting to make sense!

*(The GROUP laughs.)*

MEG. Then maybe *you've* had too much, Arthur-a-Bland!

*(More laughter.)*

MUCH. Well, *I* haven't. There's not a tooth in my head fears ale, you shinbones. You cat guts. You onion eaters.

MEG. He's a prince, isn't 'e?

MUCH. Next to you, madam, I am the King of Cows!

*(ALAN goes aside with ELLEN.)*

ALAN. Let's slip away a bit, Ellen, I'll play you a tune.

ELLEN. (*Chuckling.*) Ohhhh no. We'll be married in a week, Alan. You can wait for *that* tune.

ALAN. No. I mean, yes—No, that wasn't what I meant—

ELLEN. Father warned me about you traveling minstrels.

ALAN. (*Moves in close for a kiss.*) Well, I won't be traveling any more.

ELLEN. (*Stops him with a finger to his lips.*) Oh, Alan, why can't you get a real job? Like a miller or a tanner.

ALAN. Ellen, why just a moment ago a fellow was telling me pretty soon minstrels will be worth a fortune 'round here— Every lyric dropping like gold from their lips.

ELLEN. Fellow? What fellow?

ALAN. Good little fellow—Right there. (*Pointing across the way.*) Calls himself Lord Croop.

ELLEN. Oh, Alan, that's Much the miller. He means well, but ... well, he's given to—

ALAN. Great imagination?

ELLEN. (*Studying him with amusement.*) Yes.

ALAN. Well, that's what ya need, Ellen. Imagination. That's what gets ya places. F'rinstance now the barons are all raising their rents, right? That gives 'em more money for entertainment, right. And who do they hire for that entertainment?... Minstrels!

ELLEN. And who is that pays the rent in the first place?

ALAN. (*Pause. ALAN realizes it's them. HE thinks a moment.*) Well, that's all right! With the extra work, we'll be able to *pay* the increased rent.

(*ELLEN can only shake her head at this.*)

EADOM. Catherine! Catherine, love, fetch some more bread, will ya?

CATHERINE. Come on, Eadom, I'm entertainin' the customers!

EADOM. Let me do that an' you pump the ale!

CATHERINE. Na, I wouldn't like that nearly as much, I think.

(*Laughter from the GROUP. ROBIN, WILL, and LITTLE JOHN enter.*)

ROBIN. Three ales, keep!
WILL. I'm thirsty! Make it four!
MUCH. Five!

WILL. Six

MUCH. Seven!

WILL. Eight!

MUCH. Sold! I concede. You won fair an' square.

WILL. What'd I win?

MUCH. I don't know.

WILL. (*To Robin.*) This fellow's got a loose bowstring.

MUCH. Sir, I am not an archer and never professed to be. I am Much the miller.

WILL. Funny, you don't look like Much to me. (*WILL laughs, looking around for approval at this joke, but receiving only groans and pieces of bread tossed at him.*)

MUCH. Oh, sir sir sir, I am very disappointed. Think you be the first to make jest upon my good name? Why every bumpkin in Lincoln has done that. You are evidently a simple man. But I am not.

WILL. You have put me in my place, fair lady.

MUCH. (*To the others.*) Tell me, how long has he been out in the woods?

WILL. Too long. Can you point the way back?

MUCH. (*Backs away from Will.*) Get away from me, poor mad fellow. Why, my horse makes more sense. (*HE bumps into Little John and turns.*) Cry you mercy, it *is* my horse! I thought I left you tied up.

LITTLE JOHN. Call you me a horse, you?!

ROBIN. (*Under his breath.*) "Call you me," again—Where does he get that?

(*Grimly LITTLE JOHN lifts MUCH up.*)

MUCH. Don't be ashamed 'cause you're a horse! It's all right!

EADOM. (*Puts a tray down and approaches.*) Here now! No horseplay in here!

(*LITTLE JOHN drops MUCH and roars fearsomely at Eadom.
ROBIN hastens over to restrain him.*)

ROBIN. Don't hurt *him*, Little John, he has to serve the drinks.

(*HE and WILL take LITTLE JOHN to a bench at the long
table. THEY sit and drink ale.*)

CATHERINE. All right, everyone! More music, Alan-a-Dale!

(*ALAN begins to play. Immediately RICCON and the
ROYAL FORESTERS enter and fan out. The
MERRYMAKERS grow still and quiet.*)

RICCON. Prepare to receive the Lord High Sheriff of Nottingham!

(*The SHERIFF strides into their midst. HE surveys the room.*)

SHERIFF. Pray tell, which of you loathsome rabble is Eadom the innkeeper?

(*The GUESTS glance about warily, not sure what to do.
EADOM steps up.*)

EADOM. I'm Eadom.

SHERIFF. (*Studying him a moment.*) I hereby arrest you for non-payment of back taxes.

(*The GROUP reacts. CATHERINE steps forward.*)

CATHERINE. We try to keep up! You keep raisin' 'em—!
EADOM. It's all right, love. We'll settle this.

(*RICCON looks to the SHERIFF who nods. RICCON starts to walk slowly through the MERRYMAKERS, studying faces. ROBIN and WILL at the table, try to be inconspicuous.*)

SHERIFF. No, *I'll* settle this. You're to be made an example of. Your inn is to be confiscated in the name of the crown, and all proceeds collected thereof. And your punishment for evasion?... is death.

(*Stunned silence. RICCON nears Robin and Will.*)

SHERIFF. Take him away!

(*FORESTERS grab Eadom. CATHERINE rushes forward, screaming.*)

CATHERINE. Noooo!!

(*The FORESTERS push her down. EADOM explodes in a rage, attacking them.*)

EADOM. Leave 'er alone!!

*(The SHERIFF quickly turns and stabs EADOM. CATHERINE screams as her husband falls, just as RICCON sees ROBIN and WILL.)*

RICCON. M'Lord!!

*(As RICCON draws his sword, ROBIN and WILL topple the big table into him, also drawing swords. FORESTERS converge on them and a battle ensues.)*

SHERIFF. Arrest them all! Arrest *everyone!*

*(MERRYMAKERS scatter into the woods amid pandemonium. ROBIN and WILL, outnumbered, back from the scene, swinging swords. LITTLE JOHN, having absolutely no idea what's going on, tries to mind his own business, still seated, drinking, at the overturned table. A FORESTER grabs him and LITTLE JOHN looks at him balefully, slowly rises, and lifts the FORESTER into the air. With a roar, HE sends him flying into the other Foresters, grabs his pike and heads off after Robin and Will. The SHERIFF oversees the looting of the inn. CATHERINE is hauled away. A FORESTER drags ELLEN to the Sheriff.)*

FORESTER. What about this one, M'Lord?

*(The SHERIFF turns, about to speak, when HE is suddenly and obviously struck by her youth and beauty. HE stares at her a moment, then turns away coolly.)*

SHERIFF. Take her to the castle for questioning.

*(The FORESTER drags the protesting ELLEN off.)*

ELLEN. I've done nothing! *I've done nothing!!*

*(The SHERIFF watches her leave then turns to RICCON and
    the others.)*

SHERIFF. Fetch up everything! Come along! I want every
possession!  And find me that landlord's coffer! *(Casually to
himself.)* I have a quota to meet. *(BLACKOUT.)*

### End of Scene 4

## ACT I

### Scene 5

*AT RISE: A short time later in the area of Sherwood Forest
    known as Greenwood Glen. ROBIN, WILL, and LITTLE
    JOHN enter, out of breath from running. THEY plop,
    exhausted, before the great tree.*

LITTLE JOHN. And I thought we had it bad in Mansfield!
WILL. Aye! Sheriff of Nottingham, eh? Whattya think,
Robin, back to Locksley?
ARTHUR. *(Off.)* Who's that?! Who's out there?!
WILL. Victims of harsh injustice and cruel tyranny.

*(Pause.)*

ARTHUR. (*Off.*) What?
WILL. The rabble! The rabble!
ARTHUR. (*Off.*) Oh.

*(ARTHUR-A-BLAND, MEG SCATHELOCKE, and MUCH
enter from the woods, also panting for breath.)*

ROBIN. Greetings. Find yourself some ground. It's the
only thing that isn't taxed these days.
ARTHUR. I heard the Sheriff's working on it.
ALAN. (*Off.*) Ellen?!... Ellen?!
MEG. Quiet out there, boy! Unless ya want the Foresters
over fa tea!

*(ALAN-A-DALE rushes in.)*

ALAN. (*Rushes in.*) Who's that? Have you seen Ellen
anywhere? Ellen Deirwold?

*(The GROUP looks about.)*

ROBIN. Sorry, boy.
ARTHUR. Haven't seen her.
ALAN. Well, I've got to find 'er! C'mon, help me look,
won't you?

*(THEY look at each other with little hope.)*

ROBIN. Lad, you keep searchin' right now the only thing
you'll find is Royal Foresters. Just hope she's enough sense to
hide for the time being.

ALAN. Oh, that's not what I'd expect of men of England—
Lie down when there's work to be done.

LITTLE JOHN. Stop talking or I'll take out your jawbone.

MUCH. If you do that, he'll *never* talk.

*(LITTLE JOHN looks at Much wearily.)*

ALAN. Well, just what are we supposed to do?

MUCH. What is is, is is. So dry ya tears, my hearties.

MEG. Tears! There's no tears left in bloody England.

ROBIN. So where does that leave us? We can't cry an' we
can't run ... We must have nothin' left ta lose. *This,* my lads
an' lasses, smells like the bottom a' the barrel ta me. In which
case ... we can only go up.

ARTHUR. Oh, we will. Same like Eadom the innkeeper.
He just went up now. We'll join 'im soon enough.

ROBIN. No we won't ... Not before our time ... Not if we
stop the Sheriff and his men.

MEG. Are you mad?

ARTHUR. Oppose the Sheriff? That's what Eadom did—

ROBIN. Aye—one man ... But we're not one ... we're
many. *(Stands, looking around at them.)* And if we keep
gathering more ... and stand together—*work together* ... not a
power in all of England can stop us.

*(The GROUP looks at each other.)*

WILL. Foolish, Robin—By far the most foolhardy idea I
ever heard—When do we start?

ALAN. *(Exuberantly.)* Aye, see? Now, that's just—That's
just the kinda talk I'm talkin' about!

LITTLE JOHN. That's all it is so far ... Talk. (*HE rises and slowly walks to Robin.*) Are you willin' ta back up that talk with force?

ROBIN. (*Looking around before answering.*) Aye. (*With some amusement.*) Although ... this time not with a quarterstaff.

LITTLE JOHN.(*Stares at him and slowly gives a low, dry chuckle.*) I'm in.

MEG. Count me in, mate. What a' we got ta lose?

MUCH. Up anchor an' let's set sail!

(*The GROUP looks at Arthur. Pause.*)

ARTHUR. Well ... If you're *all* going to do it—

(*Brief cheers from the GROUP.*)

ROBIN. That's the spirit! What's ya name, squire?

ARTHUR. Arthur-a-Bland, I'm the tanner.

ROBIN. Good. We'll get ya the Sheriff's hide. You?

MEG. Meg Scathelocke.

ALAN. Alan-a-Dale.

MUCH. I'm Much!

WILL. We know, we know.

ROBIN. (*Finishing the introductions.*) Will Scarlet, Little John—

LITTLE JOHN. That's—(*HE concedes defeat.*) Mm. Little John.

ROBIN. And my name is Robin Hood.

ARTHUR. Well, *Robin Hood.* You seem to be makin' the decisions. Where do we hold up?

MEG. He's right. The Foresters'll snatch us, any town we walk in.

ROBIN. Then we won't go to a town. We'll use the forest. Greenwood Glen, right here. We'll know every inch of it. We strike quick like hawks, and then disappear into the brush.

WILL. I like this "strike," Robin, it sounds good, it sounds good. But what does it mean?

ROBIN. It means we hurt the Sheriff in his most sensitive area.

WILL. Not—

ROBIN. Yes. His pocketbook.

ARTHUR. What? Like thieves?

ROBIN. Oh, far from that, my friend. On the contrary, we're going to balance the books for him. We're going to distribute King John's wealth back to the poor people it came from.

MEG. (*Laughing.*) Kind of round about, ain't it?

ROBIN. That's right ... We're going to complete the circle.

(*Laughter from the GROUP.*)

ROBIN. First, we must enlist. A handful can't do it. Anyone we can trust, bring 'em back here—We meet at this tree.

MUCH. They call it the Sherwood King.

ROBIN. Sherwood King it is! Are ya with me?!

ALL. Aye!

ROBIN. *Then, I christen the lot a' ya—Men an' women of Greenwood! (Swords and bows are raised amid cheers. BLACKOUT.)*

**End of Scene 5**

## ACT I

### Scene 6

*SETTING: Part of the Royal Palace Garden, London. This may be placed somewhere beside or in front of the Sheriff's castle terrace.*

*AT RISE: It is some weeks later. QUEEN ELEANOR OF AQUITANE is tending her garden, pulling up weeds with a small claw. KING JOHN enters, sees her, and ducks mischievously out of sight. HE sneaks up behind her.*

KING. Boo!

*(ELEANOR doesn't react, but just keeps weeding. SHE is always the cool customer.)*

ELEANOR. Whenever I hear someone tripping lightly I just assume it's you.

KING. *(Chuckling.)* Ahhhh my very favorite mother.

ELEANOR. My least favorite son. What do you want?

KING. What do I want? Is that a way to greet a king? What do I want?

ELEANOR. *(Turning to him.)* What do you want?

KING. *(Chuckling.)* Oh, a marvelous delightful sense of humor you do have, Mum, dear Mum. *(Strolling about the garden, cheerily.)* Why you're really as bright and fresh as the flowers in your garden. How *do* you do it? Especially at your age.

ELEANOR. Weed!

KING. I beg you pardon?

ELEANOR. It's not so much a question of growing flowers as it is destroying weeds. The one negates the other.

KING. (*Stares at her aloofly. Pause.*) I see. (*Strolling again, sniffing flowers.*) If I didn't know better, I'd swear we were talking about something other than gardening.

ELEANOR. Nonsense, John, it's all just weeding. Every now and then you get one tough little bugger who refuses to come up.

KING. Very well, I'll play. Whatever do you do then, Mother dear?

ELEANOR. Only one thing *to* do. (*SHE digs the claw into the ground, demonstrating.*) Grab him right by the bulbs ... and yank!

(*SHE violently rips the weed out. JOHN's playful attitude abruptly drops.*)

KING. I think the gardening lesson is over—How quickly I tire of games.

ELEANOR. Oh, you think these to be games? I have cards up my sleeve I haven't even thought of using yet. You'd better quit while you're ahead.

KING. I've allowed the barons yet another tax increase. You know, I think they're beginning to like me more and more each day.

ELEANOR. You can give them free cows and shine their pottery for them, and the loyalty they feel for me will only grow stronger. Something you don't understand, John.

KING. (*Irritated at this.*) No. No, I don't understand it. Lion-Heart's dead, *you're* about to be.

ELEANOR. My, what sentiment. (*Pointedly, low-voiced.*) Don't count on it, John.

KING. See here, Mother, what good can it possibly do *you* to resist my invasion of France?

ELEANOR. Not me, John—This country ... Another bloody war so that you can fill your coffer?... Over my deceased corpse.

(*Pause.*)

KING. Very well.

(*ELEANOR looks at him.*)

KING. Oh no—I'm not going to kill you, Mother. The barons would never forgive me.

ELEANOR. You old sentimentalist.

KING. Yes. No, I have something much more terribly subtle in mind. Something in the nature of ... a deal.

ELEANOR. (*Chuckling.*) You have nothing to trade, Johnny.

KING. Haven't I?

(*Pause. ELEANOR continues to weed.*)

KING. What about the life of Marian Harper? She's your favorite lady-in-waiting, some might even say a friend, is she not?

(*ELEANOR's attention is now rapt.*)

KING. It seems she was involved in the murder of a Royal Forester while out hunting—Ah that firey temperament of hers. (*HE leans close to her.*) I wonder where she gets that. Of course the Sheriff of Nottingham laughed at the idea it was really her. I didn't have the heart to tell him that Marian's favorite hobby is *hunting buck* ... And that she's given to *lowly dress and buckskins*—convenient for hunting in the wood, hardly what I'd call typical lady-in-waiting. Would you, my dear?... Of course ... he could still find out ...

(*ELEANOR has risen. THEY are eye to eye.*)

KING. (*Smugly triumphant.*) I'll be calling a meeting of the barons in two weeks. If you start now, there should be more than enough time for you to send a series of messages— "Oh what a good King am I" ... and "Wouldn't it be a marvelous idea to invade France," that sort of thing. (*HE starts to leave, then turns back.*) I'd start writing soon, if I were you, dear Mum. Before all that *weeding* starts to cramp your hands.

(*HE turns and walks away, leaving a stunned and concerned ELEANOR. BLACKOUT.*)

### End of Scene 6

## ACT I

### Scene 7

*AT RISE: A short time later in Greenwood Glen, Sherwood. FRIAR TUCK, a rather stout holy man with a gravelly voice and a sword at his side, sits beneath the large tree talking to himself and eating voraciously.*

TUCK. Have some more mutton, my good man. Oh, don't mind if I do! Thank you, kind sir, and can I interest you in just a bit more malmsey? Malmsey! Why I thought you'd never ask!

*(ROBIN enters behind him, stops, and quietly ducks behind the tree, listening.)*

TUCK. And bread, perhaps? How about some bread? Oh, yes, that'll hit the spot! How polite of you, my bonny fellow! Not at all! What are friends for? Well said! Well said! (*HE roars a good-natured laugh.*) Now, you simply must try the malmsey again. Oh no, I couldn't—I insist—All right.

*(HE drinks deep. ROBIN chuckles silently.)*

TUCK. Well, in that case, you sir, should have some more mutton. Very well, if you say so! Of course, I say so. And just to wash it down—Don't tell me. Let me guess ... Some more malmsey. Just a touch. All right then, if you have another bite of mutton.
ROBIN. Thank you.

TUCK. Don't mention it. I— ... What?! (*Rising from the ground.*) Who's that spying upon me? You come out of there at once!

ROBIN. (*Crawls out of hiding.*) Good day, Friar, I meant no harm. Just thought the two of you might like some company.

TUCK. Oh— ...Now see here, rascal—My jesting is nothing to jest about. How dare you make sport of me. And behind my back.

ROBIN. (*Chuckling.*) Well it is a rather ample back, Father. Enough for two of you, I wager. And talking to yourself like that—Well, I make it at least *four* of you.

TUCK. (*Drawing his sword.*) Why you brash scalawag. I'd say a lesson's in order for you.

ROBIN. (*Still on the ground, raises his hands in defense.*) All right, Friar, all right. Henceforth, I shall never laugh at your sport. In fact, from now on I shall take all your jests quite seriously. They are nothing to joke about, it's true. Why, I'd say they're even downright sad—

TUCK. (*Putting sword away.*) Yes.

ROBIN. ... Children weeping in the streets, women tearing their hair out—

TUCK. Don't you forget it, my— ... You're sporting me again, aren't you, you scurrilous little—!

ROBIN. Oh please, good Father, I meant no harm. I've been bitter ever since ... since I lost the use of my legs.

TUCK. Your — ... (*Scrutinizingly.*) Hmmm. Sorry, fellow, I did not know.

ROBIN. Ahh it's all right, don't take pity on me. I loathe pity, Father.

TUCK. Yes, I'm sure you're used to it. What's your business here?

ROBIN. Alas, none but to leave this terrifying wood as soon as possible. But crawling thus, my progress is most slow.

TUCK. I can well imagine, my worm-like friend. Perhaps I could be of service.

ROBIN. Oh, would you? I would be ever so grateful. Do you actually think you could—dare I say it—*carry me* through the wood?

TUCK. I'm sure it's little effort.

ROBIN. You're *sure*. I mean, all that food won't explode or anything, will it?

TUCK. (*Containing himself.*) No, the food won't explode. I'm well contained.

ROBIN. Well packed, yes. (*A pathetic little chuckle.*) Like an entire winter storehouse for a family of seven hundred—you are indeed.

TUCK. (*A low mirthless chuckle.*) Well, best climb on my back now, sirrah. (*Bends.*)

ROBIN. (*Begins to climb up.*) An expanse I perceive as wide as the great Ottoman Empire itself.

TUCK. You do flatter me, sir, you do. (*Begins to carry Robin.*)

ROBIN. Not at all. Your girth has no justice, sir—nothing in the known world I can compare it to ... Except maybe ... *the known world.*

(*TUCK stops walking, doing a slow burn.*)

ROBIN. Why have we stopped, sir? We've barely progressed. The woods are still thick around us ... Although, how they seek to surround *you* is certainly one of the mysteries of nature.

*(TUCK takes a deep, grunting breath and continues.)*

ROBIN. Oh, that doesn't sound good. Surely, I've winded you. No small task, judging the amount of wind you *could* hold.

TUCK. *(Strainingly polite.)* Perhaps you could hold *yours* 'til we reach the wood's edge.

ROBIN. Oh, I don't mind. Never at a loss for words, that's me. You know—the way *you* are with *food.*

TUCK. Bless my soul! A gold sovereign!

ROBIN. *(Jumps to his feet.)* Where?!

TUCK. *(Looks at Robin's perfectly capable legs and nods, grabbing his nose.)* Right *here,* you daft little twerp! *(HE pulls, tweaking Robin's nose hard.)*

ROBIN. Ow!

TUCK. *(Smoothly draws his sword.)* Ready for a trouncing, my woodland wit?

ROBIN. *(Happily drawing his sword.)* Rather give you one, my gluttonous Friar!

*(THEY battle spiritedly. It is soon evident FRIAR TUCK knows what HE is doing.)*

ROBIN. Not bad, Your Worship! Learn this in the monastery?

TUCK. No! From parrying sinners like you, ya little heathen scamp!

*(THEY strain in a coeur-de-coeur.)*

ROBIN. Spoken ... like ... a man of ... God ...

*(THEY push off. ROBIN immediately charges back. TUCK easily bounces him off his stomach, knocking him to the ground.)*

TUCK. More solid than you expected, eh ragamuffin?
ROBIN. *(Stunned, shaking his head.)* The better to fall!

*(ROBIN, lying on the ground, hooks a foot out, tripping TUCK who lands heavily. ROBIN laughs. TUCK starts to swipe with his sword.)*

ROBIN. Hold on, Friar, hold on! I don't want to hurt you any more.
TUCK. *(Stops and lowers his sword. HE chuckles, gradually building to a laugh.)* I don't want to hurt you any more either.

*(Exhausted, THEY both sit there laughing. Robin's BAND emerges from the woods around them. The number may be increased now, if desired. TUCK looks about at them.)*

TUCK. Something tells me I've come to the right place—If this is the camp of Robin Hood.
ROBIN. It's the camp—*(Extending a hand.)* And I'm the man.

*(THEY shake hands. TUCK chuckles dryly.)*

TUCK. You're him? I should have known.
ROBIN. Welcome to Sherwood, Friar—
TUCK. Tuck's the name.

WILL. Tuck tuck tuck it away.

TUCK. (*Looks at Will disdainfully.*) Hm ... Well, I've come to join your band. If there's room for a man of the cloth.

LITTLE JOHN. There's room for the cloth ... I don't know about the man.

(*The GROUP laughs. TUCK slowly rises and walks over to Little John. HE grins, looking him up and down.*)

TUCK. If there's room enough for Galligantua ... there's room enough for me.

(*HE turns to smile at the responding laughter. LITTLE JOHN nods his head, slowly, squinting at the challenge.*)

LITTLE JOHN. No problem, Friar. We can always make the paths wider.

(*Laughter and Oooo's of approval.*)

TUCK. —Easily. I'll just grab your ankles and use you as a plow.

(*More laughter. TUCK is smug. LITTLE JOHN frowns, face working as HE tries to come up with something. The GROUP waits with great anticipation. Pause.*)

LITTLE JOHN. You just try it!

(*The GROUP laughs, including TUCK, who walks away from the grim but confused LITTLE JOHN as the CAMP starts*

*to go about its business. WILL approaches, puts a*
*consoling hand on his shoulder.)*

WILL. You lost.

LITTLE JOHN. (*Looks at him. Pause.*) I know.

ROBIN. All right, lads! Show the good friar how we work!
What have ya got? Alan?

*(As each comes forward THEY present their spoils and drop*
*them in a central pot.)*

ALAN. A lord and lady were kind enough to part with
some silver bracelets.

ROBIN. How thoughtful! Meg?

MEG. A wealthy merchant insisted we have his gold chain.

ROBIN. He shouldn't have! Arthur?

ARTHUR. This little landlord was tiring of carrying this
heavy bag of coins around—

ROBIN. (*"Moved" almost to tears.*) You helped a stranger
... Makes me proud to be your leader. Little John?

LITTLE JOHN. (*Pointedly to Tuck.*) A couple of jewelled
abbots asked if I'd care to make a contribution. I said "No,
would you?"

*(The BAND laughs, especially TUCK.)*

TUCK. Well said! Well said for my benefit, sir!

ROBIN. Will?

WILL. Coupla' sovereigns.

ROBIN. Much?

MUCH. Little.

*(Groans and cries of "Come on, Much.")*

ROBIN. All right, all right—He's trying. Carry on, Much, you'll bring something back sooner or later.

WILL. Later would be my guess.

MUCH. *(Glaring at Will.)* Good Master Robin, if I steal from one of us, does that count? *Robbing* from the poor, so I can *give* to the poor?

ROBIN. *(Puts a hand on Much's shoulder.)* Kind of ... defeats the purpose, lad, if you know what I mean.

MUCH. Then I must search elsewhere for something to bring back. The Orient, perhaps, to the land of Prester John. *(HE walks away in thought.)*

ARTHUR. *(From the edge of the wood.)* Robin, the Prioress of Kirklees.

*(The PRIORESS OF KIRKLEES enters from the wood.)*

ROBIN. Greetings, good cousin!

*(HE and the PRIORESS hug.)*

PRIORESS. And to you, good cousin.

LITTLE JOHN. *(To Tuck.)* That's Robin's cousin.

TUCK. I gathered.

ROBIN. How was your journey here?

PRIORESS. Without incident, I'm happy to report ... They tell me there are bandits in the woods.

*(SHE smiles mischievously. ROBIN grins.)*

PRIORESS. I am inclined to disagree. At least ... they've never bothered me.

ROBIN. Well, I am relieved to hear that, good Prioress. Meg, some food and wine for my cousin.

PRIORESS. Oh, I can't stay long, Robin. My duties are most time-consuming, especially in these trying times. Lately, I've had to cut back, even at the Priory. And that pains me deeply. Helping the poor is all I have in the world. Why, if it weren't for you ...

ROBIN. We do our best, cousin.

PRIORESS. Yes. You always did. Even when we were children. (*Chuckling sadly.*) And you remember how terribly poor we were then.

ROBIN. (*Chuckling faintly.*) Like it was yesterday.

PRIORESS. Now ... well, I still feel poor in a way ... Scraping to get by, avoiding the new taxes, playing political games with the Bishop on one hand, the barons on the other ... (*Wistfully.*) How I long for simpler times ...

ROBIN. We all do. But it's never simple. No matter what we change, we always long for better, I suppose.

PRIORESS. (*Pause. The PRIORESS, lost in thought, smiles.*) Well, I best be on my way. The people are waiting.

ROBIN. And they won't be disappointed—Alan?

(*ALAN has gathered up some of the booty in a satchel which HE hands to the Prioress.*)

PRIORESS. Much thanks as always. (*Seeing Friar Tuck.*) I notice you have a holy man in your midst ... I'm very pleased to see that, Robin. Good day. (*SHE nods and starts off.*)

ROBIN. Fare you well, cousin.

TUCK. (*Watching her leave.*) What does she do with the booty, Robin?

WILL. She buys ale and makes merry.

(*LITTLE JOHN hits WILL with his quarterstaff.*)

ROBIN. She distributes to the poor, part of what we take.

MEG. Aye! Under the Sheriff's very nose too!

ARTHUR. Strangers comin'! Break the camp!

ROBIN. All right, hearties! Don't leave a trace! Let's go!

(*In smooth, rapid fashion the camp is packed up and the BAND moves off silently into the wood. Pause. Voices are heard approaching. Soon, MARIAN and QUEEN ELEANOR enter strolling, plainly dressed.*)

ELEANOR. —I'm not saying you murdered a Royal Forester, my dear. But the fact you were there *can* implicate you.

MARIAN. But you talk as if I *know* this Robin Hood or something. Really, we only met once. And that, under the most unfavorable of circumstances. Why, I don't even like him—You wouldn't either, believe me. He's brash, arrogant, rude and unscrupulous.

ELEANOR. Don't leave out the horns and tail.

MARIAN. He tried to make my acquaintance under the most absurd ruse.

ELEANOR. He must have been desperate to meet you.

MARIAN. Desperate is the word. *Ridiculous* is even better.

(*THEY sit down to rest in the clearing.*)

ELEANOR. You saw through it?

MARIAN. A side of beef could see through it. Although, I'm quite sure the village maiden is absolutely thrilled by that sort of show.

ELEANOR. Well, none the less, he's gaining quite a reputation for himself. I understand the Sheriff is particularly displeased.

MARIAN. Perhaps. It's nothing to do with me.

ELEANOR. I wish that were so ... But the fact now stands, that if I don't comply with King John's wishes ... he will have you arrested and put to death.

MARIAN. I'm sorry, Your Majesty. I've put you in grave difficulty.

ELEANOR. It wasn't your doing.

MARIAN. Please. Let me take to hiding, to the woods even—I can survive. Don't let him hold my life over your head.

ELEANOR. I— ... Marian, I—I don't know—

MARIAN. It's the only way! Why, we're deep in Sherwood now. I'll stay here.

ELEANOR. In the woods? Really, dear, do you think that's absolutely safe?

MARIAN. (*Gesturing about the clearing.*) Look! Just me and Mother Nature! I'll hunt. And fish. There's not a soul around for miles!

(*Robin Hood's BAND, minus Robin and Will, emerges from the woods all around them, to stand casually watching—hands on hips, arms crossed, etc. MARIAN and ELEANOR are at first dumbfounded, then MARIAN stands, hand on sword hilt.*)

ALAN. Good afternoon, good gentlewomen. We mean you no harm.

MEG. But since you are of a class ... just a cut above the rest, we'll have to relieve you of some possessions, as it were.

ARTHUR. Spread it around.

MEG. So to speak.

TUCK. If you please.

MUCH. Don't worry, ladies! If you're lucky, you'll become poor! Then we'll give you all *sorts* of things!

*(MARIAN and ELEANOR study them a moment. Then LITTLE JOHN steps forward. MARIAN starts to draw. HE halts.)*

LITTLE JOHN. Now, there's no reason for that, good lady, no reason at all. I give you my word that no harm will come to you.

MARIAN. You're not going to harm us?

LITTLE JOHN. Not at all.

MARIAN. Your word.

LITTLE JOHN. My word.

MARIAN. (*Quickly to Eleanor.*) Good, let's go.

LITTLE JOHN. Now, hold on a second there—

MARIAN. What's the point? You're not going to harm us. You've given us your word. We might as well just go now. What's to stop us? What's keeping us here, if not fear of harm?

*(LITTLE JOHN is plainly out of his league. HE mulls this over, confused. The BAND look at one another for help.)*

ARTHUR. Alan's the smartest—Alan, bloody do somethin', will ya?

ALAN. What can *I* do? He gave his word!

MEG. Now, why'd ya go an' do that, Little John—give ya word?

LITTLE JOHN. I don't know ... I wasn't thinkin' ... I'm really not gonna harm them ya know, so don't think that for a minute, any of ya.

ARTHUR. Will ya shut up? Don't keep reassuring them, ya only make it worse.

MEG. We're losing our credibility as outlaws.

TUCK. How you people got by this long is beyond me.

LITTLE JOHN. Now don't you start, Friar, I've had enough of you.

TUCK. Well, someone better start. Now listen, ladies, either you give us your possessions or ... *(HE thinks.)* Or we'll surround you in a big clump and you'll never leave the woods.

LITTLE JOHN. *(Under his breath.)* He could do that by himself.

*(TUCK glares at him.)*

MARIAN. Fine. Fine. You do and I'll hack my way through with three feet of well-tempered steel.

*(TUCK considers this, looks to the others. The BAND huddles silently a moment, breaks.)*

ALAN. Well, wait a minute, now wait a minute, miss. That hardly seems fair. We promised not to hurt *you*.

MARIAN. Yes, you did, didn't you ... *(A broad smug smile.)* But *I* didn't.

*(The BAND look at each other. Pause.)*

    ALAN. Robin!...
    LITTLE JOHN. Robin!

*(MARIAN looks at ELEANOR at mention of the name. At this point, if possible, it would be marvelous for OUR HERO to come swinging in on a rope. If not, we'll settle for a valiant leap. At any rate; enter ROBIN.)*

    ROBIN. Welcome to Sherwood, ladies!
    MARIAN. *(Casually aloof.)* There he is.
    ROBIN. Well, it's you! How nice! I was hoping to run into you again.
    MARIAN. Your lucky day.
    ROBIN. *(Laughing.)* Ah same attitude—That's what I love about you. Men and women of Sherwood, may I present ... Marian Harper, lady-in-waiting to Queen Eleanor! And bless my soul, well this must be none other than Her Majesty Queen Eleanor herself!
    ELEANOR. Well, he seems perceptive enough.

*(The BAND laughs.)*

    MARIAN. Your Majesty, he doesn't believe you.
    ELEANOR. Well, who would. A queen wandering around out here. I hardly blame him.

*(More laughter from the BAND.)*

ROBIN. What a wonderful spirit of fun you both have! Come! You must join us, both of you! Refreshment for everyone!

*(The CAMP becomes a bustle of activity, food and drink being distributed.)*

MARIAN. Thanks, but we'd really rather not—
ELEANOR. Oh, let's stay. I'm interested to see the life of an outlaw.

*(MARIAN shakes her head as ELEANOR receives a cup of wine from ARTHUR.)*

ELEANOR. Tell me, do you really give your spoils to the poor?
ROBIN. All but what little we need for our own survival.
MARIAN. *(Chuckling.)* Yes, mere pennies I'm sure. How humble of you.
ROBIN. You could stand a little a' that yourself, M'lady. Look around.Where are the riches? The fineries?
MARIAN. Hidden from our eyes, I'm sure.
ROBIN. *(Chuckling.)* You're a stubborn little—Would you like some wine?
MARIAN. No, thank you.
ELEANOR. It's quite good.
MARIAN. Please, Your Majesty, let's go.

*(Snickers of "Your Majesty" from the GROUP.)*

ROBIN. You don't give up, do you? I do love a woman who enjoys a good jest. What do you really do? No, don't tell me. Let me guess. Tinker's wife? Pastry baker? Embroiderer?
MARIAN. Court executioner.

*(Laughter from the CAMP. WILL enters, carrying some supplies. HE sees Eleanor and drops them instantly, mouth hanging in a stupid blank look.)*

ROBIN. What's the matter, Will?
WILL. *(Slowly.)* ... Nothing ... I've ... just never seen her outside London before.
ROBIN. Who?
WILL. Queen Eleanor.

*(ROBIN nods casually with a mouthful of food. HE suddenly spits it out as the entire CAMP scrambles, getting to its knees, except WILL who remains standing numbly.)*

WILL. Yes ... I saw her once ... in London ... I really did—

*(ROBIN grabs WILL and hastily drags him down.)*

ROBIN. Forgive us, Your Majesty, we didn't—I mean, we could not—
MARIAN. Off with their heads!

*(SHE giggles delightedly but sees ELEANOR looking at her with reproach.)*

MARIAN. Sorry.

ELEANOR. Please rise um ... you ... outlaws. I never cared for that sudden attention everyone pays to the ground.

*(THEY rise.)*

ROBIN. Our humblest of pardons—
ELEANOR. It's all right. You probably don't get many queens through these parts.

*(The BAND sneaks looks at each other, unsure if this is a joke. ROBIN nods broadly and laughs. The BAND joins in.)*

MUCH. Quite a few actually—About four a day, plus a few kings—

*(LITTLE JOHN hits him. TUCK steps up to ELEANOR, presenting an arm.)*

TUCK. Your Majesty, it is indeed an honor. Even though I myself am new to this merry band, allow me to show you about the camp.
ELEANOR. Thank you. I would most enjoy seeing the operation of a bandit's lair.
LITTLE JOHN. *(Presenting his arm.)* Oh, for that you probably want *me*—

*(THEY stroll OFF with ELEANOR who takes both of their arms.)*

TUCK. She'd prefer me, lamppost.
LITTLE JOHN. You just got here.

TUCK. Yet I've learned *so* much.

*(MARIAN is about to protest, but lets her go. SHE stands awkwardly amidst the BAND who finally proceed about their work.)*

MARIAN. (*Clearing her throat.*) Tell me, outlaw, does that bow serve a purpose or is it just decoration?

ROBIN. (*Laughing.*) It serves a purpose, My Lady. Quite a few, in fact.

MARIAN. That would imply ... the user has some skill.

ROBIN. It does. It does ... Are you ... familiar with this ... skill?

MARIAN. (*Smiling coyly.*) A sight more than you'll ever be, squire. Unfortunately, I neglected to bring my bow.

ROBIN. Ohhhh miss ... You're in luck there. We just happen to have some extras.

MARIAN. (*Scrutinizes him a moment. Then SHE smiles.*) Very well, Master Hood. If only to put you in your place. I owe you a drubbing.

ROBIN. (*Bows slightly, presenting the way to the bows and arrows.*) Madam ... I accept with all my heart.

*(THEY head off in a feisty but rather pleasant mood. BLACKOUT.)*

## End of Scene 7

## ACT I

### Scene 8

*AT RISE: The following day on the great hall terrace of the Sheriff's castle, ELLEN DEIRWOLD wanders about, as perturbed as SHE is bored, desperate to remove herself from a difficult situation. SHE sighs in defeat. Then with sudden desperation, SHE bolts to the wall of the terrace, attempting to climb over. HILTON enters, sees ELLEN, and rushes over, hauling the struggling girl back in.*

HILTON. No, you don't. That'd be all I'd need—You fall and get yourself hurt or killed. How would that look for me? Huh?

ELLEN. I hadn't considered that, to be honest with you.

HILTON. (*Plops her onto a stool.*) Ahh I can't figure you. Chance of a lifetime for a good-for-nothing little serf, and you don't even realize it. If he'd asked me, I'd have married him like *that*.

ELLEN. Be my guest! Go ahead! Take him away! Sweep him off his feet!

*(The SHERIFF enters.)*

ELLEN.—You have my blessing!

*(THEY see the SHERIFF who just stares at them.)*

SHERIFF. Hilton, you may go.

*(HILTON leaves awkwardly. The SHERIFF looks at ELLEN a moment. HE walks about.)*

SHERIFF. Your disposition doesn't seem to be improving ... If it makes a difference, I've spoken to your parents and they've given us permission to wed.

ELLEN. No, they didn't.

*(Pause.)*

SHERIFF. Well, I don't need their permission anyway—I'm the Sheriff.

ELLEN. Upholder of the law.

SHERIFF. Well, what do you want me to do? Woo you?

ELLEN. Oh, please don't do that. Please spare me a wooing.

SHERIFF. Frankly, I wouldn't know how to.

ELLEN. Frankly, I'm not surprised. And I appreciate that, by the way.

SHERIFF. *(Looks at her a moment, then grabs her roughly.)* My, but you do—

ELLEN. Let me go!

SHERIFF.—You do have a sharp tongue for a little ragamuffin whom I had the generosity of dragging up from the mire.

ELLEN. You! You'd have me *deeper* in it!

SHERIFF. *(Slaps her.)* See? You see what you've made me do? *(HE strolls about.)* Oh, this had better improve, that's all I can say. When we're married, my dear, your attitude had better change. *(HE leans across the table to her, quietly.)* Or I really will visit your parents ... And it won't be so much *asking* for *your* hand ... as it will be *removing theirs.*

*(ELLEN studies his cold malevolence fearfully.)*

SHERIFF. Hilton!

*(HILTON enters quickly.)*

SHERIFF. Take her.
HILTON. The Bishop, My Lord.

*(HILTON takes ELLEN out, passing by the BISHOP OF HEREFORD who watches them leave with amusement.)*

BISHOP. ... Made in heaven.
SHERIFF. There are more important things—
BISHOP. I know. Robin Hood struck again.
SHERIFF. Robin Hood! All I hear is Robin Hood!
BISHOP. He's becoming more famous than King John.
SHERIFF. Rob from the rich so he can give to the poor! What kind of nonsense is that?! Doesn't he know I'm only going to take it away again?! Hasn't he heard of taxes?!..Idiots!..If this absurd recycling of funds continues, I might as well burn the bloody books!
BISHOP. Sort of clever when you think about it. Amusing little serfs. Seems like they're always up to something—
SHERIFF. Oh, Hereford, I'm glad you can take this so lightly. Have you forgotten the taxes go to your church too?
BISHOP. Of course not, I never forget money. I just don't worry about it. That's the difference between you and me. You agonize and bang your head—I'll continue to spout pleasantry and good humor.

SHERIFF. (*In a rage.*) And in doing so provide none of the assistance of the "valuable ally" you're supposed to be!!

BISHOP. There they go again. Those horrid veins ...

SHERIFF. Bishop!!

BISHOP. Now it just so happens I have given the matter some thought. And if you calm down, I just might tell you about it.

SHERIFF. (*Exhales. Pause. HE plops down in his chair with weary resignation.*) Grace me with your brilliance ...

BISHOP. Gladly. Now it seems to me, that if we deprive the dragon of its head, it will cease to breathe fire and smoke.

(*The SHERIFF slowly, balefully, turns to him, then looks away again.*)

BISHOP. Now. I have always said, "To catch a thief, it takes a thief."

SHERIFF. (*Disinterested.*) Have you.

BISHOP. It just so happens, in my native Herefordshire there is a bold and murderous outlaw of great renown, of equal cunning and notoriety to this ... Robin Hood. He has done me many a favor in the past ... for the right price.

SHERIFF. And what might that be?

BISHOP. Two hundred pounds should attract his interest.

SHERIFF. (*Turns to him sharply. Pause.*) It had better do more than attract his interest. I would expect nothing less than Robin Hood's head on a pole.

BISHOP. (*Staring at him.*) I find this preoccupation with the human bonnet disgusting to say the least. I shan't be here for the delivery, I promise you.

SHERIFF. (*Rises, strolls in thought.*) Tell this brigand we will pay him half now and the other half upon completion of his task.

BISHOP. I'm sure he'll be agreeable. You'll find him a strange sort of fellow, as feared by the people of my region as Robin is loved by his. (*Leans forward with melodramatic amusement.*) He wears the hide of a horse ... He *believes* it gives him power.

SHERIFF. He can wear daisies and a dunce cap for all I care, as long as he gets the job done. What's his name?

BISHOP. Guy. Guy of Gisbourne. (*BLACKOUT.*)

## End of Scene 8

## ACT I

## Scene 9

*AT RISE: It is one week later, somewhere in Sherwood Forest, away from Robin's camp. MUCH enters, singing the traditional "Spotted Cow" in his usual merry fashion.*

MUCH. "Good morning to you wither? said I! Good morning to you now! The maid replied, kind sir, she cried! I've lost my spotted cow! No longer weep, no longer mourn! Your cow's not lost my dear! I saw her down in yonder grove—" (*As HE refers to the woods in mid-song, HE halts suddenly. A FURRY SHAPE, apparently an animal, is stirring the bushes, grunting.*)

MUCH. You're no cow ... Identify yourself, animal, if you're a member of that family as I perceive you are. (*HE begins to creep closer*.) A wolf? A bear, perhaps—although that I do not hope. You're not a fish, unless fish has fur and rabbits swim the sea.

(*HE jumps as the FIGURE suddenly turns and rears up on two legs, with a terrifying roar. It is GUY OF GISBOURNE. HE is big and bearded, wearing the toughened hide of a horse, complete with ears and mane. His roar turns into a hearty, robust laugh.*)

GUY. Hello, little fellow!  Say, did I scare you? I didn't mean to do *that*.

MUCH. (*In awe.*) You—You can talk.

GUY. Talk!... Well, of course I can talk ... Can you?

MUCH. I was worried. I thought you might be a bear at first.

GUY. A bear! (*HE laughs.*) Imagine a bear talking!

(*HE laughs again. MUCH hesitates, then joins in. GUY abruptly stops, eyes popping.*)

GUY. I'm a horse!

(*MUCH stares. GUY stomps and whinnies.*)

MUCH. You are! You are a horse! I'm certainly relieved at that.

GUY. Aye, so am I.

MUCH. Wait'll my friends see you! You know, I never bring anything back to camp. But now—

GUY. Friends? Camp?... Well what can this mean, little neighbor?

MUCH. Oh, I'm not supposed to talk about that. (*Suspiciously.*) Unless you're all right ... Do you think you're all right?

GUY. Oh, I'm better than all right. (*Whispering slowly.*) I'm looking for the camp of Robin Hood. Have you heard tales of him, little man?

MUCH. Oh ... mayhap I have ... In one form or another.

GUY. Aye, lad, and many such forms he takes, I've heard tell. This Robin is, a one-eyed ogre with skin like bark, one day—and a gold-spitting hag, the next. And his merry band fly through the forest on wings of silk, and live in the ground in mighty caves, drinking blood by the light of the moon.

MUCH. (*Pause. MUCH is spellbound. HE turns to no one in particular.*) This horse has some strange notions.

GUY. Ohhh methinks not, little—What's ya name?

MUCH. Much.

GUY. Much. Why I would *fain* have to see it for myself ... to not believe the tales I've heard ... These aren't just horse's tales. (*Pause.*) Ya get it?... *Horse's tales*?

(*MUCH is blank. GUY roars at him.*)

GUY. Tales?! Tales?! Tales?!

MUCH. Tales!

GUY. Exactly.

MUCH. Well, I—I—I—I—don't know

GUY. (*Expansively.*) What's to know, little man? (*HE pulls out a wine sack, sets himself comfortably on the ground, gesturing for Much to do the same. Cheerily.*) Now let's have a swig of satisfaction, a merry ol' time, a bevy of song ... (*Extending the wine sack to Much.*) ... and talk of Robin Hood.

*(MUCH stares at the wine sack. BLACKOUT.)*

## END OF ACT I

## ACT II

### Scene 1

*AT RISE: Somewhere in Sherwood Forest. No time has passed since the previous scene. It is quiet for a moment then ROBIN and MARIAN enter skulking, armed with bows and arrows. Their hunt has now become a regular event. THEY rush to some cover. Their speaking is hushed.*

ROBIN. Shhhh! Be quiet!
MARIAN. If you *talk* you're not being quiet.
ROBIN. Then, why are you talking?

*(THEY look at each other with equal reproach, then go back to waiting.)*

MARIAN. I suppose this is how you wait for unsuspecting maidens.

ROBIN. ... Well, I ... don't usually shoot them with a bow and arrow, but ... yes, this is the general approach.

MARIAN. (*Shaking her head.*) And he's proud of it. Truly unbelievable.

ROBIN. Well now, I don't always use "The Rescue" *of course.*

MARIAN. (*Astounded and amused.*) "The Rescue"!... You mean, you have a *name* for it?... Like it's a form of *dumb show*?

73

ROBIN. Well, it *is*! It's entertaining, isn't it?

MARIAN. Well, it *is* dumb.

ROBIN. Yes— ... Here now, if it's so dumb how is that my lady-in-waiting happened to fall for it?

MARIAN. *Fall* for it! I did nothing of the kind! And I'm not your lady-in-waiting.

ROBIN. Thank God for small blessings—

MARIAN. I saw through that childish ploy right from the start.

ROBIN. You ate it up like mutton.

MARIAN. Oh, really! What an imagination! Not to mention an insufferable ego to match that of King John.

ROBIN. Here now, watch that tongue.

MARIAN. Why? Will you put an arrow through me?

ROBIN. I'd rather put one through that deer, but you just scared him off.

MARIAN. (*Quickly alert.*) What deer?!... I don't see it!

ROBIN. Gone a mile now. You scared the antlers off him.

(*MARIAN stops straining to see it, realizing SHE's been hoaxed. SHE pushes ROBIN over, grinning.*)

MARIAN. Scared the antlers off *you*, more like.

ROBIN. No, it wasn't the antlers.

(*MARIAN chuckles slightly, ROBIN suddenly tenses.*)

ROBIN. Here! Listen! Now we got a real one!

MARIAN. (*Grinning.*) Really, how gullible do you take me, sir knave?

*(SHE pokes him repeatedly in the ribs. HE grabs her playfully.)*

ROBIN. Any way you'd *like* me to ... my lady ...

*(THEY kiss. Voices suddenly come from the other side of the wood. ROBIN and MARIAN freeze. HE motions and THEY scurry off. The voices are of the BISHOP OF HEREFORD and a FORESTER, who enter.)*

BISHOP. You call this a road? This is not a road! Oh God! Oh God! It's more like the bottom of a river or something. Can't you clear this—this ... *stuff* out of my way? These ... *branches* and *twigs* ... like the infernal tendrils of hell reaching up to drag me down, to deprive the gentle Earth of this abundance of holiness—

FORESTER. I thought you wanted a shortcut.

BISHOP. *(Stops to rest.)* No. What I wanted was for you to fix the wheel of our coach.

FORESTER. I couldn't lift it by myself, could I, Your Grace. P'raps if you'd lent your back to the task—

BISHOP. *"Lend my back."* How disarmingly funny you are for a Forester. You're only trying to cheer me up. I haven't "lent my back" to anything since climbing on a swing as a child—Actually, I was helped up—Are you sure this the right way to the Sheriff's castle?

FORESTER. Aye, M'Lord.

BISHOP. It is most inconvenient. Why can't he visit Hereford once and a while?

FORESTER. I'm sure I can't imagine, M'Lord.

BISHOP. Yes, I'm sure you can't. Oh, God, I'm certain my death is imminent. Even now, I can feel its cold icy hand upon my brow—"Come with meeee. Come with meeee," it's saying. I might as well walk with my own head in my hands and offer it to the highest bidder.

FORESTER. Your Grace should try to keep his lid *on*.

BISHOP. Oh, very funny. Stop trying to cheer me up, it won't work. You'd do better to kill me with your sword before somebody else does.

FORESTER. Is that an order, Your Grace?

BISHOP. Of course it's not an order, you ninny!

FORESTER. Oh. Good thing I didn't carry it out then, isn't it.

BISHOP. Good thing for your sake ... If you understood what a *figure of speech* is ... Well, I suppose you wouldn't be a Forester then, would you.

FORESTER. No. (*Pause.*) I'd be a bishop.

BISHOP. Oh, shut up. Shut up and let me die free of levity. Once the soil gently drums the lid of my coffin, you may jest all you want.

FORESTER. Thank you, M'Lord.

BISHOP. Are you sure this is the right way? Oh, I can't stand this! know I shall die of heart attack long before the bandits find me! That's some consolation at least. Promise me you won't let them desecrate my person.

FORESTER. Aye, I'll threaten 'em, M'Lord. All hundred of 'em. Come along.

*(The rest over, THEY start to walk again. WILL steps out from the wood before them. The BISHOP shrieks.)*

WILL. Sorry, Your Grace. Didn't mean to startle you.

BISHOP. A minion of Beelzebub!

FORESTER. 'Ere you. What's ya business, 'ere?

WILL. Business? (*Pause. WILL thinks.*) Oh, I know. Pies.
FORESTER. What?
WILL. (*Calling as a vendor.*) Pies! Any fine pies today!
BISHOP. No, we don't have any pies. What would a
bishop be doing with pies?

(*Pause.*)

WILL. No no no no. *I* have the pies. See, I'm sellin' 'em.
Listen— (*Calling.*) Pies! Who will buy my fine pies, today?!
Pies!
BISHOP. Get out of the way. We don't want your fine
pies. Where do you keep them anyway, in your pockets? Let's
go.

(*LITTLE JOHN steps out beside WILL. Now the two of them
bar the way. The BISHOP yelps.*)

LITTLE JOHN. What's the trouble here?
BISHOP. We're trying to pass, but this ... pie salesman
won't let us.
LITTLE JOHN. Ohhhh no! Not the pie man again! He's
always doing this!
BISHOP. Really? It's annoying.
LITTLE JOHN. Certainly is. Now see here, you, that's a
full-fledged bishop right there. Do you know you're blockin'
him?

(*Pause.*)

WILL. Pies! Who will buy my fine pies today?! Pies!

*(THEY begin to push LITTLE JOHN's quarterstaff back and forth in an extremely mock struggle. ARTHUR enters.)*

ARTHUR. All right, break this up now! What's this all about?

BISHOP. The pie man's annoying everyone because we won't buy his pies.

ARTHUR. Doesn't seem right at all, does it?

LITTLE JOHN. Well, instead a' talkin', why don't you help me move 'im?

ARTHUR. Needn't be cheeky about it.

BISHOP. He didn't mean it—Would you *help*!

ALAN. (*Enters from the woods.*) Here, I'm tryin' ta pass, do you mind?

BISHOP. Well, we all mind, but it won't do any good.

WILL. Pies! Who will buy my fine pies!

BISHOP. Perhaps if one of you bought one from him—

LITTLE JOHN. *You* buy one! You look like you've had the practice.

BISHOP. (*To the Forester.*) Did you hear what he said to me?!

FORESTER. I'm sorry, I haven't kept track, M'Lord.

*(MEG enters from the woods.)*

BISHOP. Not another one!

MEG. What's all this noise 'ere? You're disturbin' the woods.

BISHOP. There's nobody *left* in the woods!

MEG. What goes on 'ere?

LITTLE JOHN. (*Slowly, broadly long-suffering.*) We're trying to move the *pie* man.

WILL. Who you pushin'? Don't push the pie man.

BISHOP. *Kill* the pie man.

ALAN. Try *lifting* him maybe. We'll go under.

BISHOP. Who *are* all these people?

MEG. Divide the pie man in two—We'll go between him.

BISHOP. I had no idea this forest was so busy.

ARTHUR. Reason with the pie man. He'll understand that.

BISHOP. They should make the road much wider at this spot.

WILL. Look, all I wish in life is to sell my good pies.

MEG. Ohhhh, why didn't you say so!

ALAN. I'll buy a pie!

ARTHUR. I'd like a pie very much.

LITTLE JOHN. I'd like *two* pies.

BISHOP. What *is* this? It's too confusing. Wait! Are you all in this together? Is this a trick to get me to buy a pie? All right, all right, I'll take one! Let me have a pie! Let me have *all* your pies!

*(The BISHOP is now surrounded, leaving the FORESTER out of the group. LITTLE JOHN grabs the FORESTER by the collar, quietly.)*

LITTLE JOHN. If you run away really fast, I won't rip your ankles off.

*(Pause.)*

FORESTER. Fair enough.

*(HE runs off. The BISHOP is engulfed in a veritable tide of outlaws.)*

BISHOP. What are you doing? Careful! I'm very holy!

*(FRIAR TUCK enters.)*

BISHOP. Oh, thank goodness—a good stout monk! I hope you are flesh and blood and not some trick of the wood sprites.

TUCK. I'm real enough, fatty.

BISHOP. Oh, thank G— ... *Fatty!*... What man of God calls me fatty?

TUCK. A true man of God. One not so richly dressed.

BISHOP. *Thus* am I closer to God. Who can be richer than that?

TUCK. We can ... After we help ourselves.

*(Laughter from the BAND.)*

BISHOP. To what abbey do you belong, sir?

TUCK. To the Abbey of Sherwood.

BISHOP. I know of no such abbey. Who is your abbot?

TUCK. Friar Robin Hood.

*(Pause. The BISHOP screams, fainting back into the BAND who catch him and hold him up. The BISHOP recovers with a series of panting sobs.)*

BISHOP. Please! Please! I'll pay you! I'll make you all rich men!

*(ROBIN swings/leaps into the scene.)*

ROBIN. Ya hear that, lads?! We can be rich! Just like him!

BISHOP. Yes! Yes!

ROBIN. Hundreds of Bishops of Hereford, marching down the street! Covered in jewels! Our fat bellies jiggling in the wind!

WILL. I don't know, Robin. Doesn't sound too good.

BISHOP. Robin!

ROBIN. Ahhh, now think it over, lads an' lasses! It would give us a chance to be cruel and merciless and have all the food we can eat—depriving those less fortunate, through higher taxes.

BISHOP. Yes! I mean, no—

ROBIN. (*Moves closer to the Bishop, quietly.*) You mean *yes* ... Because that's the way you think ... You're selfish and greedy and ignorant. You give nothing to the people, but your loathing. You're the least holy man I know, besides King John.

BISHOP. He is a personal friend of mine.

ROBIN. (*Smiling ominously.*) I know ... I have considered that ... in your sentencing.

BISHOP. Sentencing!

ROBIN. Yes ... But, I'm leaving you to a higher judge.

BISHOP. (*Eyes wide.*) ... I—I think I know who you mean!

ROBIN. Really? I'm surprised at that. He's forsaken you long ago. As you've forsaken him.

BISHOP. What—what are you going to do?

(*The PRIORESS enters a ways behind ROBIN. SHE sees the Bishop and ducks out of sight, but not before the BISHOP sees her.*)

ROBIN. First ... I'm going to give you a chance to say your prayers—if you still remember how ... Then ... *we're going to hang you!*

BISHOP. No! No! No! You can't! You can't!

*(The BISHOP is quickly blindfolded and a broken noose is placed around his neck.)*

BISHOP. I tell you, you're making a mistake!

ROBIN. No, I think we've got it right—noose, neck, tree, drop—I think that should do it. Take this walking pillow to the nearest branch and heave him! Farewell, Your Grace! It's been unpleasant!

*(The BISHOP is whisked off.)*

BISHOP. No! No! No!...

*(MARIAN steps out of the woods beside the grinning ROBIN.)*

MARIAN. *(Not without amusement.)* Naughty, naughty. You're a cruel man, Robin.

ROBIN. I've been taught by the best ...

*(OFFSTAGE we hear a chant of "One! Two! Three!" The BISHOP screams, followed by gales of laughter. The PRIORESS steps out.)*

ROBIN. Cousin!

PRIORESS. Yes. I just saw what you did. Harsh—but I suppose he had it coming.

ROBIN. What? (*Pause*.) Oh, no— ... You thought— ... Prioress, you didn't really think we'd *hang* him.

(*Pause.*)

PRIORESS. Oh. No. No, of course not. I meant, your *prank,* it's a harsh *prank* to play.

ROBIN. Yes, of course.

(*Awkward pause.*)

ROBIN. Oh. Marian Harper, may I present my cousin, the Prioress of Kirklees.

PRIORESS. Charmed—Robin, if it's all right with you, I'd better take my charity and leave. It was a trying journey.

ROBIN. Of course.

MARIAN. The booty *really* is distributed to the poor?

PRIORESS. (*Sharply.*) What a thing to say. Why wouldn't it be?

ROBIN. (*Chuckling.*) Oh, this lady had her doubts, that's all. But I'm sure you've convinced her, Prioress.

MARIAN. (*Sighing mischievously.*) Oh, I suppose. (*BLACKOUT.*)

## End of Scene 1

## ACT II

## Scene 2

*AT RISE: Meanwhile, elsewhere in Sherwood Forest MUCH
and GUY continue to drink and make merry, singing the
traditional "Treadmill Song."*

MUCH AND GUY. "Step in, young man, and know your
fate. It's nothing in your favor. A little time I'll give to you.
Six months unto hard labor. With me—Hip! for the day.
Me—Hip! for the day." Me—Hip! for the day, for the day-de-
ohhh ..."

GUY. "At six o'clock the screw comes in—"

MUCH. "... a bunch of keys all in his hand!"

GUY. "Step up, my lads, step up inside—"

MUCH AND GUY. "... and tread the wheel 'til breakfast
time!"

*(THEY burst into laughter. GUY slaps Much hard on the
back. HE suddenly becomes serious.)*

GUY. (*A quick bark.*) You're off-key!

MUCH. I'm sorry, horse, I never professed the singing
ability of a four legged animal.

GUY. Well who would? (*Passing Much the wine sack.*)
Tell me more of this Robin Hood. It must be a right merry
camp to live in.

MUCH. I fain think it is, good my horse.

GUY. Fain?

MUCH. I fain think—

GUY. Fain fain fain, why are you all fain? Strike that word from my sight and never thus utter again!

MUCH. Fain?

GUY. (*Roaring.*) *Strike,* I say! Rid yourself of such frills and humbuggery! No pretensions and no affectations! *Strike!!*

MUCH. Aye, my captain, strike will I.

GUY. (*Bends close to Much, quietly.*) Now ... *Where,* Much—*where* exactly is this happy camp?

MUCH. Camp, my horse? What camp?

*(Pause.)*

GUY. (*Smiles, batting his eyes.*) Why, the bandits' camp.

MUCH. Bandits, my horse? What bandits?

GUY. (*Roaring.*) Robin Hood!! Robin Hood!! Give to the rich!! Take from the poor!! Where's the bloody camp!! The camp of Robin Hood!! (*Quiet and pleasant again.*) Do you know the one I mean?

MUCH. I fain think so—

GUY. Strike!!

MUCH. I mean ... I think so. It's yonder about two miles. Follow the stream upland. It comes to Greenwood Glen. There's a stand of oak and beech. That's the camp.

GUY. *(A broad smile.)* Ahhh ...

MUCH. (*Tentatively.*) Good horse ... art thou ... *mad* at me?

GUY. You? Mad at *you*? My good little friend? Of course not.

MUCH. Oh.

GUY. (*Brightly.*) I'm just *anxious.*

MUCH. Oh ... 'Cause in all my experience, I never did meet a horse what was mad.

GUY. (*Carefully.*) Oh ...?

MUCH. Aye. All even and pleasant-tempered they are. Why, it's the gentlest animal in the world.

GUY. So I am, so I am.

MUCH. No, you're not ... You're mad as a hatter ... And I *fain* wonder ... if I am mad too ... for telling you what I done told ...

(*GUY appears menacing a moment, as if HE's about to strike, but instead HE bursts into the "Treadmill Song" again.*)

GUY. "Now Saturday's come, I'm sorry to say—"

MUCH. (*Sings very nervously as HE begins to slowly back away.*) "... for Sunday is starvation day."

GUY. (*Moves toward the terrified MUCH.*) "Our hobnailed boots and our tin cups too—"

MUCH. "... they are not shined and they will not—" (*BLACKOUT.*)

## End of Scene 2

## ACT II

### Scene 3

*AT RISE: On the terrace of Nottingham Castle, the SHERIFF is putting up with the BISHOP, who, as usual, is on the divan.*

BISHOP. They wore the hides of large animals and I swear some of them still had the entrails left inside, so foul was their stench. Many of the bandits had eyes removed and teeth missing with fingernails like long claws scraping on the ground. As they tortured me they laughed like banshees and feasted upon live insects.

SHERIFF. No small children?

BISHOP. Do you want to hear the tale of my exploits or not?

SHERIFF. I wouldn't miss this for the world.

BISHOP. Good ... One of them was a giant—an ogre who caused rockslides whenever he spoke.

SHERIFF. Rockslides—

BISHOP. Yes. Another was a false holy man, a monk from the caves of Satan himself—an immensely fat and disgusting person, I assure you.

SHERIFF. Yes, I can almost see him.

BISHOP. What? Yes. Well, after torturing me for hours they finally decided to end their orgy of pleasure by hanging me—an act I was sure would bring me instant relief. But even this solace was not allowed me. Such was their state of poverty and disarray that the rope was quite old and ill of quality. It snapped clean away.

SHERIFF. Perhaps the strain was too much.

BISHOP. Oh haw haw, it was a cheap rope.

SHERIFF. Yet they didn't try again. Why?

BISHOP. It was obvious ... They had no more rope.

SHERIFF. Then why didn't they try another method?

BISHOP. Great cavities in their skulls revealed that many of their brains had been removed. By habit or accident, I could not tell.

SHERIFF. (*Sneering.*) Their brains had been removed— Yes, that's why they constantly outwit us. So the rope broke and you outran them, is that it?

BISHOP. Worse, they—Such was their utter disregard for my person that they walked away ... *Laughing!*

SHERIFF. You poor man.

BISHOP. Yes! It was awful! So cruel!

SHERIFF. Hereford, you overstuffed cushion! If they had wanted to kill you, they would have! Can't you see they only wanted to scare you? To show you they're not afraid of us?

BISHOP. I escaped through God's will.

SHERIFF. God hasn't listened to you for decades.

BISHOP. I can see further conversation is futile. I have related my adventure and that is that. These monsters must be stopped at all costs. Especially this loathsome Robin Hood.

SHERIFF. What was he like?

BISHOP. I was not impressed. By his bearing, his manner of speech—I was not impressed.

SHERIFF. And when do we hear from this Guy of Gisbourne?

BISHOP. Shortly, I expect. But like a cooking pot he cannot be watched in hopes that he will boil—

SHERIFF. Shut up.

HILTON. (*Enters.*) My Lord, Guy of Gisbourne.

SHERIFF. (*Snidely to the Bishop.*) I think I hear the pot whistling now. (*To Hilton.*) Send him in.

(*GUY enters abruptly, flustering HILTON.*)

SHERIFF. You may go.

(*HILTON and GUY walk out.*)

SHERIFF. Not you, Gisbourne! (*To the Bishop.*) Are you sure about this?

BISHOP. He's eccentric.

GUY. (*Returns.*) Thank you, thank you, Your Majesty. Most gracious.

SHERIFF. I am not Your Majesty.

GUY. Whose majesty are you?

SHERIFF. (*To the Bishop.*) Two hundred pounds? Two hundred pounds for a clown? For a court jester in a horse's costume?

GUY. (*Mewling pathetically.*) Oh, Majesty, your little words sting me.

SHERIFF. (*At the door.*) Someone remove this pathetic wretch from my sight!

*(GUY suddenly spins the SHERIFF around.)*

GUY. (*Grim intensity.*) Wretch? ... Jester?... Clown?... No one talks to me like that ... And this is not a costume. This is the hide of a horse, tanned and cured—tough as armor, but lighter still—through which the strength of the horse is passed to me. I have slain three score men, which Robin Hood will be one more, and any who doubt ... *oppose me now.*

*(Pause.)*

SHERIFF. If you ever touch me again your head will leave your shoulders so fast you'll be able to watch it hit the ground. Once this job is complete you'll never set foot in Nottingham again, is that clear?

*(Pause.)*

GUY. (*Slowly smiles.*) Clear ... Clear, clear and mostly clear, Your Majesty.

SHERIFF. I am not— (*Gives up correcting him.*) What progress have you made?

GUY. Oh, that which is best, have I made, sir. The camp of which location, I have in my hands.

SHERIFF. And where is this camp?

GUY. (*Laughing.*) Oh, I think not. Have an armed force march in there and scatter the lot? A *hundred* muddy the water that *one man* treads clearly. Besides ... that wasn't the agreement. It's a head you'll be gettin' and not a drawn map.

SHERIFF. Very well.

GUY. Two hundred now and another two when I deliver.

SHERIFF. (*Slowly.*) You're holding me up? You're holding me up for more?

GUY. Now that I have the location, yes.

SHERIFF. Which of you is Robin Hood?! I can no longer tell!

GUY. Come, come, Lordship, I know what this man means to you both. I heard they robbed some fat bishop just the other day. (*HE laughs.*) And mighty God, ya shoulda seen Hereford blubber an' sweat when he commissioned me! What a sight!

(*HE chuckles again. The SHERIFF slowly turns to glare at the squirming BISHOP.*)

THE BISHOP. I was only trying to peak his interest.

SHERIFF. (*Fuming, writes on a piece of paper. HE hands it to Guy.*) Take this deposition to my attendant.

GUY. (*Smiling, bowing, exiting.*) Thank you. Bless you, Your Sweet Kind Gracious Majesty. Lord of all the Earth and

that which is more. Sovereign of the Realm of Darkness—
(*His voice trails off as HE departs.*)

SHERIFF. (*Looks at the Bishop.*) That's the last time you ever buy horses for me.

BISHOP. ... Oh, yes! I see your jest—

SHERIFF. Quiet!... Are there any warrants pending on Guy of Gisbourne?

BISHOP. I usually just tear them up. The Sheriff of Hereford is a friend of mine. And believe me, warrants for Gisbourne come as frequently as rain. More so in fact, now that I think of it—it having been a rather dry season, at least in Heref—

SHERIFF. Hold the next one and have it delivered to me. When Gisbourne hands me *Robin's* head ... I will hand him *his own.*

(*The SHERIFF smiles. The BISHOP chuckles.*)

BISHOP. That's what I like about you, you have a marvelous sense of fair play.

SHERIFF. Now for our ... surprise guest. (*At the door.*) Send her in!

(*HILTON enters escorting the PRIORESS OF KIRKLEES.*)

SHERIFF. Thank you for waiting, Prioress.

PRIORESS. What is this about, Lord Sheriff?

BISHOP. You know full well what it's about, my dear.

SHERIFF. Come, come, you were in the bandits' camp, were you not?

(*Pause.*)

PRIORESS. I see no reason to deny it. It is God's will I was born Robin Hood's cousin, and no doing of my own.

*(The SHERIFF and the BISHOP are stunned.)*

SHERIFF. *Cousin ... There's* an interesting shade of color ... If ever there was a threat to your ... *retaining* the priory at Kirklees, I would say it was ... *blood ties to a murderous outlaw.*

PRIORESS. Murderous ... You know he's not murderous—

SHERIFF. No! Not when it's a Royal Forester—

PRIORESS. Not when it's self-defense!

SHERIFF. Oh please ... I did not bring you here to discuss legalities. The situation is plain ... You are doling out stolen money given you by Robin Hood. More than enough to pack you from the priory and slap you in prison for good ... Unless of course—

PRIORESS. Unless what?

SHERIFF. You see, Lord Bishop? She's eager for a chance to make good. *(Quietly to Prioress.)* I knew you had some in you ... You are to report to me Robin Hood's every move. From now on I want to know everything these outlaws do. Is that clear?

PRIORESS. Yes. It is.

SHERIFF. You comply very quickly. Have I reformed you so fast? I warn you, if you try any sort of trick—

PRIORESS. *(An ironic chuckle.)* No, My Lord. You didn't reform me. The donations from Robin Hood? I keep half that money for myself ... You see, I'm not as strong as my cousin. And in these sad times with our serpent King John—

SHERIFF. Take care—

PRIORESS. ... draining the kingdom dry, the only way I could keep the priory going was through a little thievery of my own ... No, you haven't reformed me ... (*Quietly as SHE heads out.*) I was at your level to begin with. (*SHE exits.*)

(*The SHERIFF not quite expecting that, looks at the Bishop. BLACKOUT.*)

## End of Scene 3

## ACT II

### Scene 4

*AT RISE: Later at Robin Hood's camp, an evening of eating, drinking and merriment is in progress. A fire would be nice but not necessary. MARIAN is present. ALAN-A-DALE plays a cheery tune. WILL is drunk.*

WILL. Play "Seventeen Come Sunday"!
ALAN. That *was* "Seventeen Come Sunday."
WILL. Play it again.
MEG. Too bad Much ain't here for this.
ROBIN. Where is Much?
LITTLE JOHN. Ain't seen him for days.
WILL. Ahh you know him—His drawbridge only goes halfway.
LITTLE JOHN. At least he's *got* a drawbridge.

WILL. (*Stares at him. The battle is on.*) I'd need one too, if I had a moat like *yours*.

LITTLE JOHN. Why would you need a moat, your walls are so low anyway.

ROBIN. (*Slowly.*) What are you two talking about?

(*Pause. WILL and LITTLE JOHN look blank.*)

WILL. Castles.

ARTHUR. (*Rushes into camp.*) Robin! Two things! First, there's a man approaching from the north, headed right for us.

ROBIN. One man?

ARTHUR. Aye. Never seen 'im before.

LITTLE JOHN. Break camp, Robin?

ROBIN. No. No, let's see who he is. What's the other thing, Arthur?

ARTHUR. My turn on watch is over, can I have something to eat?

(*Jeers and food objects fly at Arthur.*)

ROBIN. Alan, keep playing. Everyone else uh ... be merry.

(*The camp comes to life again and GUY OF GISBOURNE slowly wanders in. All eyes watch him in the casual manner of any group to a stranger. GUY suddenly raises his hands and the MUSIC stops. Silence. GUY recites.*)

GUY. I walked a mighty way today. To peep in a fairy dell. Just to watch the dear little gnomes at play ... And see them work as well. (*Pause.*) A cheery good evening to you all, good sirs and— ... lasses! Well, bless me, I never expected to find lasses in a den of robbers and thieves! Tell me, which one of you is Robin Hood?

LITTLE JOHN. Robert who?

MARIAN. No, he said Robin Hood—You know.

ROBIN. (*A bit of the silly twit.*) Oh, yes! He's the famous outlaw, isn't he? I've heard some *smashing* things about him.

TUCK. I'm afraid you have us mistaken, good sir. I am Friar Tuck and this is my flock. We were just having a midnight mass.

GUY. And I am Philip of France come to eat British soil from a bowl. Is King John about?

*(Some laughter from the CAMP.)*

WILL. He's a *jolly* one, isn't he? You're a *jolly* fellow!

ROBIN. Yes, well I suppose we might as well tell you the truth. It's plain you're onto us.

GUY. Yes, sir.

ROBIN. We're not here for a midnight mass ... We're a band of traveling gypsies—*Play, Alan!*

*(ALAN plays gypsy music on the lute, and most of the BAND jump into made-up folk dances—none of which are alike— while ROBIN and MARIAN stand smiling at Guy.)*

GUY. What good luck! I'm a gypsy too!

*(GUY joins in the wild dancing much to the chagrin of the others who gradually stop until GUY's the only one dancing. HE bursts into laughter.)*

ROBIN. You're a very *strange* gypsy, aren't you.

GUY. Ahh Much was right! Dear Much—He told me you liked a good jest!

LITTLE JOHN. Much who?

WILL. Much what?

ROBIN. How Much?—I mean—Who is this Much person?

GUY. All right, gentlefolk, play your game. I understand. I'll not crack your parapets—

WILL. That's a relief. (*HE shrugs a "this one's crazy" to the others.*)

GUY. I know how risky it is being an outlaw. In all of Herefordshire there's none as feared as Guy of Gisbourne.

ROBIN. Ohhh, yes. Robs from the rich so he can rob from the poor.

GUY. Nooo, pure fancy, sir. Rumors and mythological interpretations. When you get famous, the mouths of the countryside feel they have their way with you. (*HE sits quietly, helping himself to an ale.*) Saddens me, sometimes it does ... Good brother Robin gleans the good news ... whilst poor Guy of Gisbourne suffers the bad ... Maybe if I were prettier ...

WILL. (*Mock tears.*) That's so sad.

(*MARIAN shoves him.*)

ROBIN. We never turn away a good man. Stay the night and sup with us, Gisbourne.

GUY. You are kind, good sir.

TUCK. Tell us, good fellow, what means that hide you're wearing?

GUY. This ... is the hide of a horse. It's strength is passed through me.

TUCK. Mm interesting. Little John's got the head of an ox—We don't know what passes through *him!*

*(The BAND laughs. LITTLE JOHN threatens with his staff a moment. GUY is serious.)*

GUY. I assure you, good people ... the power of the horse ... is nothing to joke about.

*(Pause. ALAN plays quietly and the camp returns to normal activity, but wary of the newcomer. ROBIN sits beside him.)*

ROBIN. Tell me, Guy, where is this ... Much fellow you spoke of?
GUY. Oh. Wandering ... Here. There. Everywhere ... *(HE chuckles.)* You know him— *(Turning casually away from Robin.)* Robin ...

*(ROBIN looks at him blankly. BLACKOUT.)*

### End of Scene 4

### ACT II

### Scene 5

*AT RISE: Early the following morning somewhere in Sherwood, not far from the camp, ROBIN and MARIAN*

*are lying peacefully in the grass, their scabbards off to one
side.*

MARIAN. You really want to hear it, don't you?

ROBIN. Well, I wouldn't mind hearing *something,* at least.

MARIAN. Well, I don't know if I particularly want to *say*
it.

ROBIN. Why not?

MARIAN. Well, for one thing, the sole purpose seems to
be to assuage your massive ego.

ROBIN. I think it's rather *your* ego that's at stake, don't
you? When someone can't do a simple thing like admit they
made a harsh, irrational judgement on another human being—

MARIAN. How can you say that? (*Softly, close to him.*)
Especially in light of what's happened ... I should think after
last night—

ROBIN. Now, wait a minute here, don't try and buy off my
feelings ...

*(Pause.)*

MARIAN. What does that *mean*? What are you *talking*
about?

ROBIN. Well, it's obvious, I'm just trying to separate
work and pleasure. I know you respect me in one area ... it's
... the other I'm concerned about.

MARIAN. (*Pause. Stares at him.*) You mean I respect your
pleasure, but I don't respect your work?

*(Pause.)*

ROBIN. Well, it sounds foolish now, of course.

MARIAN. I'm glad we agree.

ROBIN. But you know full well what I mean.

MARIAN. No I do not, Robin. I do not separate a person from what they do. In this life you are as good as your deeds. And I wouldn't have ... (*Pause.*) ... *you know*, if I didn't ... think, um ... uh ... *well* of you.

ROBIN. Oh, that was well put. You left out more words than you put in.

MARIAN. I was wrong about you, *Robin!* I was wrong about you, *Robin Hood!* Takes from the rich, so he can give to the poor! Ballads will be sung, banners will be raised, and food will be named after you. Children will look up, the Sheriff will look down, but you will always look straight and true. Long live your name and may all your offspring be giants—Have I left anything out? Was that what you wanted to hear?

(*Pause.*)

ROBIN. Yes. Yes, I think that rather does it.

MARIAN. (*Pushes him over.*) You are such a ... Saxon.

(*HE grabs her playfully. After a moment, THEY kiss. GUY appears, moving stealthily behind them through the woods.*)

ROBIN. What did you mean Saxon?

MARIAN. Oh, Robin, you—

(*SHE gives a quick cry as SHE sees GUY emerging from the woods. ROBIN is on his feet, but their scabbards are not within reach.*)

GUY. Sorry, gentlefolk. It seems I've made the first error of a wandering woodsman ... Never come upon a lad and his lass. (*Pause.*) Unless, of course, the lad's not around! (*HE roars laughter.*)

ROBIN. (*Warily.*) What can we do for you ... Guy?

GUY. Oh, nothing really. I'm an early riser, especially when you sleep in a strange camp—You know how that is? Someone else's camp? (*HE shudders.*) I don't know what it is. Somebody else's grass, somebody else's rocks—Makes you restless, I suppose. I'll probably just hunt for some breakfast. (*HE stretches.*) Aye, that sounds like a hearty, robust idea— Hunt for breakfast. Man needs the kill, I suppose; the fresh scent of blood and meat ... Doesn't he, Robin.

ROBIN. I never said my name was Robin, friend. You did.

(*GUY chuckles, taking a step forward. ROBIN backs gradually away. Throughout the following, a careful cat and mouse begins.*)

GUY. What *is* your name?

ROBIN. I never did say.

GUY. Never did say—That's a fair, bonny lass you got, lad, I swear. She looks high-born. Is she high-born?

MARIAN. Low-born. Born in a pond.

GUY. (*Impressed.*) In a *pond.* Aye ... (*Chuckles.*) And I thought you were a fairy princess ... Never knew a real fairy princess.

(*ROBIN suddenly goes for the swords. GUY rushes over to cut him off. ROBIN freezes. GUY laughs. Then HE slowly* takes a small mace from his belt, smacking it into his heavy gloves.)

GUY. What I want to know is ... How hard is Robin Hood's head? Will it crack like an acorn?... Or a walnut?

(HE suddenly lashes out. ROBIN dodges as GUY smashes the ground. MARIAN rushes for the swords, but GUY jabs the mace at her. SHE stops. HE chuckles—almost a low growl—truly in his element. ROBIN is on one side now, MARIAN on the other. GUY, in between, stands on the swords, jabbing back and forth from ROBIN to MARIAN. THEY feint, trying to reach their swords. As GUY jabs at Marian, ROBIN signals to her, pointing to the swords.)

ROBIN. Save yourself, Marian! Run!

(SHE bolts. GUY focuses on ROBIN, coming at him, swinging at his legs. ROBIN dodges, avoiding the blows. MARIAN suddenly stops and runs back to the swords, which are now unattended. GUY turns, sees this, rushes quickly over and jams his boot down on one of the swords as MARIAN grabs the other. SHE tries to pull it from the scabbard, but GUY is upon her and SHE stumbles backward. MARIAN tosses the scabbard over GUY to ROBIN who catches it and quickly unsheathes it. GUY turns from the unarmed MARIAN as ROBIN slashes at his chest. The sword glances harmlessly off the tough hide. GUY laughs and pulls a dagger from his belt and THEY square off. ROBIN parries blows from the mace and swipes of the dagger as GUY forces him back, brutally battering his sword. MARIAN now snatches up the other sword and

*swipes at Guy's back just as HE knocks ROBIN down with
a mighty blow. Unharmed, GUY spins, slaps Marian's
sword away with his mace, and raises it high for a crushing
blow. ROBIN is up and hurls himself at GUY, knocking
him to the ground with a hard check. GUY drops the mace
and scrambles to pick it up. Before HE can, ROBIN leaps
on his back, locking his arm around Guy's throat. GUY
bucks, trying to throw ROBIN off. HE does and ROBIN
tumbles to the ground. GUY rises and, with his back to us,
raises his dagger above ROBIN. MARIAN swipes at the
back of Guy's legs and HE buckles, giving ROBIN enough
time to pick up the mace and smash GUY twice in the face.
GUY freezes a moment, then falls forward upstage onto his
face. ROBIN and MARIAN on all fours, gasp for breath.)*

ROBIN. Are—Are you all right?
MARIAN. Yes ... You?
ROBIN. I'm all right. (*ROBIN plops, face down.*)
    MARIAN. Me too. (*SHE collapses, exhausted.
BLACKOUT.*)

## End of Scene 5

## ACT II

### Scene 6

*AT RISE: Days have passed. We are at Tanner's Grove in
Sherwood Forest, ROBIN enters cautiously with sword
drawn. HE halts and crouches, listening. Hearing*

*something from the direction HE just came, ROBIN ducks
into the brush and waits. Pause. MARIAN and WILL enter.
ROBIN emerges.*

ROBIN. What are you two doing here?

MARIAN. No, the question is, what are *you* doing here?

WILL. Aye, why so secretive, Robin?

ROBIN. If I'm secretive, don't you suppose I might have a
reason?

MARIAN. Yes. We just felt it might not be a good one.

*(Pause.)*

ROBIN. All right. It's my cousin. She's in deep trouble.
The Sheriff and the Bishop found out what she's been doing.
They *know* we're related. They're threatening her with prison if
she doesn't comply with their wishes. Poor thing's frightened
to death. She sent me a message to meet her here at Tanner's
Grove. Right now, she doesn't trust anyone but me, that's why
I had to come alone.

WILL. Fine. What shall we do?

ROBIN. You're going back—That's what *you* do—

WILL. Aw now wait a minute, Robin, ya big bloody
hero—

ROBIN. She'll panic if she sees more than me—Now off
with ya, the both of ya.

WILL. Well, what if we—?

MARIAN. You heard him, Will, he's got to go it alone ...
You know how he's always *right*.

ROBIN. Yes, it's annoying, isn't it?

*(MARIAN doesn't listen. SHE drags WILL and THEY head back off the way they came. ROBIN crouches and waits. Pause. A stirring causes him to tense. The PRIORESS emerges from the woods. ROBIN stands.)*

ROBIN. Prioress. Over here.
PRIORESS. Robin! I'm so glad you came.
ROBIN. You've nothing to fear, cousin. I'll protect you ... The Sheriff will not harm you, I give you my word.

*(Pause.)*

PRIORESS. *(Slowly.)* Robin ... I fear you are right ... You *will* protect me ...

*(ROBIN puzzles this odd statement. But only for a moment; ROYAL FORESTERS, led by RICCON, emerge from the surrounding wood and quickly subdue the surprised ROBIN. His sword is ripped from his grasp and RICCON backhands him. ROBIN stares at the PRIORESS in disbelief.)*

PRIORESS. I—I'm sorry, Robin. Survival has never been ... an easy thing. As I told you—difficult times.
SHERIFF. *(Enters, cheerily.)* Come, Prioress. Let's not dampen an otherwise triumphant occasion with maudlin sentiment and half-hearted excuses—You betrayed him ... and *he* will die. There! You see how simple it is?
PRIORESS. I have done what I have done. Listening to you was not part of the bargain.
SHERIFF. Careful, Prioress, I could still change my mind. *(HE approaches the restrained Robin.)* So, the merry bandit of

Sherwood himself. We finally meet. I hope it's as great a pleasure for you as it is for me.

ROBIN. Only if you run yourself through with a sword a number of times, Lord Sheriff—

SHERIFF. (*Swats him across the face.*) So bold, the outlaw—So arrogant ... That will change.

*(Suddenly MARIAN and WILL charge in, swords drawn.)*

WILL. Don't despair, Robin!! Help is fast approaching!! Ya-haaaa!!

*(RICCON smites Robin with the butt of his sword to free up himself and the FORESTERS who meet the challenge. The SHERIFF draws his sword and clashes with WILL. MARIAN spins about, parrying the others.)*

WILL. Norman swine!! Prepare to meet thy doom!! You jackals and pomegranates!! You deceptive deceivers of deception!! Such trickery!! Such rude manners!! Such ... vertigo!! I am heady with the drink of battle!!

SHERIFF. You are heady with the butt of malmsey, you illiterate little hobo!! You pathetic little tramp!! You have challenged the finest swordsman in the Kingdom!! Poor choice for a practice bout!!

WILL. (*Laughing.*) I won't need the practice where *I'm* going!! (*Realizing the mistake of this statement.*) No, *you* should say that to *me*—I won't need practice to slice you up, you lump of talking cheese!! You loosely strung vegetable puppet!!

*(Far outnumbered, MARIAN is disarmed, but not before wounding two of the FORESTERS. WILL and the SHERIFF continue to battle furiously.)*

SHERIFF. Keep spouting the nonsense, ragamuffin, it compliments your dueling style!!

WILL. Ha!! You haven't *seen* my dueling style!! I don't *have* a dueling style!!

*(The SHERIFF is getting the upper hand, backing WILL towards a tree. MARIAN watches, held by the FORESTERS.)*

MARIAN. Will, run off!! It's no good!!

WILL. He who fights and runs away ... won't get a chance like this again!

SHERIFF. Bravely spoken!

*(The SHERIFF stabs WILL, pinning him to a tree. MARIAN gasps, stops struggling.)*

WILL. Oh ... I think I'm dying. A glorious end ... Too bad Robin didn't see it.

*(HE dies. The SHERIFF sheathes his sword.)*

SHERIFF. If only he was as quick with the sword as he was with his tongue, I might have had a match on my hands. *(HE turns to look at Marian.)*

MARIAN. *(Slowly, coldly.)* You will regret what you have done this day.

*(Pause. The SHERIFF slowly walks to her.)*

SHERIFF. *(Amused, quietly.)* Until that *most fearful* time
... take her away.

*(The FORESTERS start to do so. BLACKOUT.)*

**End of Scene 6**

**ACT II**

**Scene 7**

*AT RISE: The following day at the Royal Palace Garden,
London. KING JOHN enters, creeping mischievously,
peering about for Eleanor. Pause. ELEANOR quietly but
casually enters behind him. JOHN calls softly singsong.*

KING. Mother! Oh, Mother!

ELEANOR. Trying to find a good tree, John?

KING. *(Startled, then chuckling.)* Really, Mother, I'd
hardly classify you as a tree. Old, perhaps, but not a tree. And
it is *you* that I am looking for, Mother dear.

ELEANOR. How interesting, John, seeing as I was
looking for you this very same time.

KING. Most delightful of coincidences—We have found
each other! You know I am constantly enchanted with life's
little organizations as if we're all players in the cast of some
marvelous mystery play. You, the kindly aged queen mother,
ever watchful of her favorite son's fortunes—Me, the

beneficent young potentate gazing out over a sea of sublime worshippers who bask lovingly in his glow. His brow, deeply furrowed with concern for their well-being, even as his eyes twinkle with the love that only a shepherd knows for his helpless flock. His face shining down upon them like a great smiling sun from a very high place. The lowly come from miles around to kneel at his feet—or as close as they're allowed to get—and give thanks ... just to be alive in his realm ... "Thank you King John! Thank you!" they say ... *"Thank you ... for being our king."*

*(Pause.)*

ELEANOR. Are you sure this was a mystery play and not a farce?

KING. (*Looks at her with slight reproach that breaks into a smile.*) Oh, Mother, you do jest well. Why absolutely nothing will blight the rays of this smiling sun today.

ELEANOR. (*Coming close to him.*) Nothing?... Let's try shall we?

KING. (*Hint of nervousness.*) Whatever do you mean, my dearest giver of life? I trust ... this has nothing to do with your ... persuasion of the barons. We ... had an agreement there—an understanding—

ELEANOR. Have some clouds passed in front of the smiling sun?... Or is this a *total* eclipse?

KING. W—W—W—What could you be saying? Has something changed that I should know about?

ELEANOR. The sun that sees all? I can't imagine. I would have thought news travelled to you faster than a fleet of fish-wives.

KING. Pray, what news?

ELEANOR. ... That Maid Marian Harper has been arrested for complicity with Robin Hood and they are both to be executed. On the Sheriff's wedding day, if you can believe that.

KING. What? No.

ELEANOR. Yes ... Your light is dimming, oh luminous one.

KING. Why, that can't be. I—It's a mistake, just a mistake, I assure you.

ELEANOR. Then I suggest, His Highness correct it.

KING. Yes ... I will ... I'll go there at once. Rest assured.

ELEANOR. I don't think I will. I think I'll go with you.

KING. Oh. Yes. Quite. I'm sure the Sheriff will be honored.

ELEANOR. He'll squirm in his breeches and you know it. I'll rather enjoy that. Come, let's away.

*(THEY start to walk off.)*

ELEANOR. Tell me, what do you wear to a combination wedding and execution?

KING. Well, I—I don't know really. I don't think I've ever—

ELEANOR. I suppose black would do.

KING. Yes, yes, that would be nice—

ELEANOR. Or perhaps red, for blood.

KING. Well— ... yes, that I'm sure that sounds ... fine ... *(BLACKOUT.)*

**End of Scene 7**

## ACT II

### Scene 8

*AT RISE: Days later on the terrace of Nottingham Castle. The SHERIFF storms about while ELLEN sits.*

SHERIFF. This is not working. It just isn't working. I don't know if even a barony is worth putting up with the likes of you. I assumed a simple rustic farm girl would present few problems. Simple! Ha! Nothing pleases you! Nothing placates you! You are stupid, stubborn and pigheaded! I wonder if I have not done this Alan-a-Dale a favor. The idea of doing anything for the bandits of Sherwood causes me utter loathing at the very thought. (*Coming close to her. Quietly.*) I've a good mind to give you back. That'd show them.

*(ELLEN cannot hide pleasure at the thought she might be winning.)*

SHERIFF. But I won't ... I'll break you yet ... If I have to use sterner measures.
    ELLEN. *What is it* that you want of me?
    SHERIFF. I did want your love, your respect ... (*Slowly.*) But I'll settle for your obedience. You'll quickly learn you have seen the Lord High Sheriff in his grandest of moods ... Are you prepared for the worst?
    ELLEN. (*Studies him closely. Then SHE looks away coolly, speaking quietly.*) I'm marrying you, aren't I? I have no choice. What more must I do?

SHERIFF. For starters ... you can *smile*. To anyone!
Everyone! A polite, warm, friendly, unpretentious smile—
Especially to King John.

ELLEN. You smile at him, blow 'im a kiss if you like—I
don't feel like it. That's all you really care about, isn't it? Your
Royal Acceptance. A farm girl, a commoner that you've made
decent, to parade before the court like a puppet. A simple,
wholesome baroness for the newly appointed baron ... Well,
your titles and your gold and your power only make me dirty.
Do what you want to me, I'll never smile at black Prince
John.

SHERIFF. (*Leaning close to her.*) If I promise not hunt
down Alan-a-Dale and hang him by the neck ... will you smile
at King John then ... my dear?

(*HILTON rushes in just ahead of KING JOHN.*)

HILTON. His Royal Majesty King J—

KING. I hate to break up this tender romantic interlude—
(*Whispering, pointing to the door.*) It's Mother! She's—

(*QUEEN ELEANOR enters. The KING abruptly goes into an
act as HILTON removes ELLEN.*)

KING. How dare you! How dare you keep Queen Eleanor's
favorite lady-in-waiting, Marian Harper, here against her will!

SHERIFF. (*Dour, chagrinned sarcasm.*) How could I have
done such a thing?

KING. I don't know. Perhaps you have taken leave of your
senses.

SHERIFF. Perhaps I have.

KING. I should have your job.

SHERIFF. I wish you did.

*(The KING shoots him a look, then continues. HILTON reenters.)*

KING. Dare you to hold her prisoner?! Why it's as obvious a case of mistaken identity as ne'er I seen! Even the court fool could see that.

SHERIFF. *(Under his breath.)* Apparently he has.

KING. I demand you release her at once! Do you hear me?!

SHERIFF. Fairly well.

KING. I *demand* it!!

SHERIFF. Very well, My Royal Liege. I shall deliver this poor wretch at once into Her Highness' custody. However could I have done this?

*(The KING gives him a subtle look of warning against going too far.)*

SHERIFF. A thousand pardons to both Your Majesties and any other Majesties I might have discomfitted by this outrageous and unforgivable behavior.

*(The KING clears his throat.)*

SHERIFF. I only hope I may live a thousand years so I may repay this debt ten thousand times over—provided you live so long as to collect it.

KING. Yes, thank you, Sheriff, that will do.

ELEANOR. *(Applauding.)* Thank you both. A sad yet happy ending to a touching and beautiful play. Now that we've wept, where is she?

SHERIFF. My attendant will have Marian Harper released in your royal custody, Your Highness. Hilton?

HILTON Yes, My Lord?

*(Pause. The SHERIFF stares at her.)*

SHERIFF. *(Reiterating with impatient gestures.)* Have Marian Harper released in the Queen's royal custody.

HILTON Oh, aye My Lord. This way, Your Majesty.

*(HILTON and ELEANOR exit.)*

KING. Played that a bit thick, didn't you? Not that I'm a critic of these sort of things.

SHERIFF. Just once ... Just once do you think you could shine the torch of your knowledge in my direction so that we don't tread each others' toes in the darkness of my ignorance.

KING. Now you're being melodramatic.

SHERIFF. *I'm* being melodramatic! What about, "How dare you, how dare you" for the benefit of the Queen?

KING. The Queen and I have an agreement concerning Maid Marian.

SHERIFF. But did you think to tell me? No!

KING. It didn't concern you.

SHERIFF. As it turned out, it *did*!

*(Pause.)*

KING. Do you want your bride to be taller than you at the wedding?

*(The SHERIFF glares a moment, then sits.)*

KING. Good. Now, I'm just dying to meet this Robin Hood and I want you to be in your usual high spirits.

SHERIFF. (*At the door.*) Have Robin Hood brought in!

KING. Don't you think executing him on your wedding day is just a trifle morbid?... Oh well, it's your happy occasion, not mine. Tell me, how is he as a prisoner?

SHERIFF. How is he as a prisoner? We have tea at four and after that a game of chess—How should I know how he is as a prisoner? I'm not the bloody jailer.

KING. You *could* be ... You know what I'm talking about, Lord Sheriff ... Have you broken his spirit?

SHERIFF. (*Looks at him a moment.*) I shall. He's just a man.

KING. He's a commoner. Commoners lead hard lives. They are used to mistreatment. It is becoming so everyday to them, I fear they may build up an immunity. We may be turning them into supermen.

(*RICCON HAZEL enters dragging in a chained ROBIN HOOD whom HE throws roughly to the floor.*)

RICCON. Robin Hood, M'Lord!

(*ROBIN looks up at them, filthy, haggard, and in some discomfort. The KING strolls over for a closer look.*)

KING. He doesn't look like a bandit chief.

RICCON. Now he's the chief of the rats, M'Lord. Only they don't pay 'im much mind.

*(RICCON chuckles harshly. The KING looks at him with distaste..)*

RICCON. *(Stops chuckling and clearns his throat.)* I was just about to give 'im 'is daily lashin', M'Lord.

SHERIFF. That honor will have to wait 'til later.

ROBIN. *(With effort.)* Later! You can't rearrange my day like that. You'll throw off my entire schedule.

*(RICCON swats him.)*

SHERIFF. Pathetic fool  That's right, make it worse on yourself ... This, my annoying little pest, is *King John.*

KING. This annoying little pest is King John? How does Your Majesty allow a mere servant to talk to him like that?

*(ALL are stunned and the SHERIFF slaps ROBIN who jumps up to throttle him and has to be restrained by RICCON.)*

KING. Had a good breakfast, did he?

SHERIFF. If that tongue were removed, it wouldn't be so quick.

KING. Maybe you'd be able to keep up with him then.

SHERIFF. Ha!

ROBIN. *(To the Sheriff.)* Well said, My Lord.

SHERIFF. I grow tired of this carnival atmosphere. Does Your Majesty wish any more of this ... entertainment? Or shall we send for the jugglers and turn the great hall into a circus?

KING. I'll turn it into a tinker's shop and stable, if I so choose.

SHERIFF. By all means, bring in the horses and the tinkers!

KING. I would keep this Robin Hood around if I were you! He keeps you on your toes!

ROBIN. I've earned him a barony—Why not?

SHERIFF. Oh, look what he's doing—Trying to turn the two of us against each other.

KING. What utter nonsense!

SHERIFF. Why, he's making a fool of Your Majesty!

KING. You're the one who's falling to pieces!

SHERIFF. *I* am!

KING. Yes, look at you! Raising your voice! Turning red as a beet!

SHERIFF. So are you! So are you!

KING. I—

*(The KING catches himself. HE and the SHERIFF both calm. Pause. The KING looks eye to eye with the defiant ROBIN.)*

KING. You are a clever fellow, aren't you?... You know, maybe I was wrong. Perhaps it is a good idea to have an execution at the wedding ... I think I'll rather enjoy it. *(BLACKOUT.)*

**End of Scene 8**

## ACT II

### Scene 9

*AT RISE: The bandits' camp, Sherwood. ROBIN's BAND sit about, sulking in a quiet gloom. Long pause. Finally ARTHUR jumps up full of hope, trying to egg them on.*

ARTHUR. Look, when ya think about it, need we really be so gloomy, lads?!

ALAN. (*Glumly hopeless.*) Ellen's to marry the Sheriff tomorrow.

ARTHUR. Aye, but we'll find a way out of that!

MEG. (*Forlornly.*) Much is dead.

ARTHUR. Aye, lads, I know, but we must press on.

LITTLE JOHN. Will is dead.

ARTHUR. Well ... aye, I know but ...

TUCK. Robin and Marian are to be executed tomorrow.

ARTHUR. (*Growing gloomier.*) Aye ... Aye, that's true ...

MEG. And King John will ruin all England in his war against France.

*(Pause. ARTHUR glumly sits back down.)*

ARTHUR. Aye, well since ya put it that way ...

*(Pause. A stirring gets their attention and MARIAN quickly enters.)*

ALAN. Marian!

TUCK. However did you escape, dear lady?

MARIAN. I ... know some people.

MEG. Oh, aye! A queen! That usually helps.

TUCK. Unfortunately all Robin knows is a bunch of ragged, uncouth, ill-mannered, hobgoblins who run around in the woods.

*(LITTLE JOHN glares at him a moment.)*

TUCK. I'm including myself, of course.

LITTLE JOHN. Of course.

MARIAN. We must act quickly, if we're to have Robin and Ellen Deirwold.

ALAN. Aye!

ARTHUR. Aye, we must!

*(Pause.)*

TUCK. But ... what'll we do?

LITTLE JOHN. You load of oats, it's simple, mind you!... We come up with a *plan*!

ALAN. Aye, a plan! That's it, a plan! What's—What's the plan?

*(The BAND looks at each other to see if there's a plan among them. Pause.)*

MARIAN. I'm waiting ... I don't exactly hear the twang of bowstrings. 'Cause if no one shoots, *I've* got a few arrows in the quiver.

LITTLE JOHN. What's she talkin' about?

MEG. I think she means she's got an idea—Although why she couldn't *say* that ...

TUCK. We'd—We'd be grateful if you do, My Lady. Y'see ... Robin was always good at that sort of thing—coming up with plans and such ...

MARIAN. Gladly, Tuck. I've learned the layout of the Sheriff's castle ... I think we can free Robin under the Sheriff's very nose ...

ALAN. And Ellen?

MARIAN. That ... will be the second step ... *(BLACKOUT.)*

## End of Scene 9

## ACT II

### Scene 10

*AT RISE: The following day at Nottingham Castle. The MUSICIANS play triumphant but slightly martial fanfare. A ramp has now been placed, leading down from the terrace to the ground below where a long table has been set up, loaded with fare—of which the BISHOP partakes with relish. RICCON and the FORESTERS watch jealously from behind him, along the base of the wall. The PRIORESS enters and chats with the BISHOP, quite liking her new place in the world. KING JOHN enters with the SHERIFF, and HILTON in tow. The KING stops chatting when HE sees the FORESTERS below.*

KING. Eat! Eat! Eat! This is a festive occasion! All you want—courtesy of Your Lord High Sheriff!

*(RICCON and the FORESTERS virtually pounce on the food, elbowing the BISHOP out of the way.)*

KING. That's the way. Look at those healthy appetites. They *would* have *fought* for you ... *Now* they'll *die* for you.

SHERIFF. I'll never understand your logic.

KING. I fear that may be so.

BISHOP. (*Approaches them in disarray.*) May it be that you go too far in this? Or do my very eyes deceive me? Common soldiers like ruffians eating at the same table as I? Men of ill manner quite like savage beasts—I swear one of them rubbed his shoulder against mine—A bishop, mind you! Don't you have a trough or something? Some sort of wallow? Perhaps *I* should join the pigs—I think they're more *refined* than the Foresters. Why, they don't even know I'm holy.

SHERIFF. Who? The pigs?

BISHOP. Not the pigs ...

KING. My Lord Bishop, right now we have more important matters to discuss than table manners. The Queen is procuring the support of the barons. Very soon we shall embark on a great adventure and I'm going to need both of you behind me.

BISHOP. I'm not going to war, am I? I don't travel well and I fare very poorly in battle—We have priests who do that sort of thing.

SHERIFF. Quiet, you ninny, he's not talking about that. Monetary support, am I right, Your Majesty?

KING. (*Smiling.*) Exactly  ... My Lord Baron.

*(The SHERIFF smiles. ELEANOR and MARIA enter from the great hall. THEY nod curtly to the KING and his entourage and proceed down the ramp toward the table.)*

ELEANOR. I am absolutely famished. Would you join me in a bite, my dear?

MARIAN. I think not. Perhaps later I'll be of ... stronger appetite.

ELEANOR. Of course.

SHERIFF. Where are your three monks? Why are they not here yet?

BISHOP. They'll be here. They're nauseatingly dependable. I can think of no other reason to have monks at a social gathering except to perform a ceremony. Have you ever feasted with them? Very dull fellows, absolutely no sense of humor.

PRIORESS. Well, you look quite fine, Maid Marian. A far cry from the woods of Sherwood, isn't it? There's really little one can appreciate about the hard life.

MARIAN. Yes. Luxurious surroundings are a comfort I ... couldn't go without for long.

PRIORESS. ... Thus your return to the courts and castles ... Despite the fact you're in love with my cousin?

*(Pause.)*

MARIAN. In love? *(A low chuckle.)* Dear Prioress, a mere trifle. But then, what could you know of such things? I made good use of this ... outlaw ... just as you did.

*(MARIAN walks away, coolly watched by the PRIORESS.)*

BISHOP. Shouldn't we have the bride brought in? Is her father here to present her?

SHERIFF. No.

BISHOP. No?

SHERIFF. No.

BISHOP. Why not, might I ask?

SHERIFF. Because I don't need him, that's why! He's not giving her away—Don't you understand? I'm taking her! I'm taking her!

BISHOP. Well, who's going to present her? Someone must present her.

SHERIFF. Didn't I tell you? You are—Now go and fetch her.

*(Flustered, the BISHOP exits. The KING and ELEANOR have been watching.)*

ELEANOR. I love weddings, don't you?

KING. Terribly romantic.

*(THREE HOODED MONKS enter and HILTON confers with them, then turns.)*

HILTON. May I present three holy brothers of the Abbey of the Fountain Dale!

SHERIFF. Yes, yes, bid them approach.

HILTON. This way please.

1ST FRIAR. (*Ancient, querulous voice.*) Thank you. Bless you.

*(HILTON leads the MONKS up the ramp to the Sheriff.)*

SHERIFF. My bride will be along shortly— ...Would someone tell the Foresters to stop eating please.

*(RICCON nudges them and all gather round the foot of the terrace.)*

SHERIFF. Now. Which of you will perform the ceremony?

1ST FRIAR. I am he, My Lord, and these are my retainers.

SHERIFF. Very well. (*Pause.*) Well, why don't you prepare or something?

1ST FRIAR. Prepare, My Lord?

SHERIFF. Yes ... Something holy ... Don't you have a ... book or something?

1ST FRIAR. I need no book, My Lord. I memorized the ceremony many years ago.

SHERIFF. Yes, about a hundred, I'll wager—Where is my bride?!

*(Enter the BISHOP with ELLEN in bridal gown.)*

BISHOP. We're coming—You'll ruin the splendor if you keep yelling.

*(The MUSICIANS strike up a march. The BISHOP leads the gloomy ELLEN down to the Sheriff. The KING turns to Eleanor.)*

KING. She looks marvelous, doesn't she? Like a deer caught in a torchlight.

SHERIFF. Here is my lovely bride.

1ST FRIAR. (*Examining the Bishop.*) She's well jewelled, I see, but this gown makes her wider than a moat. Ever miss a banquet, my dear?

SHERIFF. That's My Lord Bishop!

BISHOP. (*Blusters of indignation.*) Where did the Abbot find you—in a catacomb?

SHERIFF. *This* is the bride!

1ST FRIAR. Oh my. It *is*!... Why, she looks so sad. I do perceive lilies in her cheeks instead of blushing roses.

SHERIFF. Is he a monk or a florist?

1ST FRIAR. (*Pinching Ellen's' cheek, as to a child.*) Is this a bonny bride? Is this a bonny bride?

SHERIFF. Quiet, you doddering fool! Perform the ceremony!

1ST FRIAR. She's not a bonny bride at all, no no no no no—

KING. I think this fellow had some ceremony before he came here.

1ST FRIAR. (*To the Sheriff, again as if to a child.*) Does this girl truly love My Lord Sheriff? Come on, little fellow, tell the truth now. A monk knows when your lyyy-iiing.

SHERIFF. Hold that insolent tongue or I'll cut you in two!

1ST FRIAR. What if I don't want to hold your tongue—? (*To Ellen.*) Do you really want to marry this greasy toad?

ELLEN. As a matter of fact ... no, Your Grace.

1ST FRIAR. I now pronounce you ... unmarried.

SHERIFF. You say yes or I'll carve you up in an instant!

(*HE grabs her as the 1ST FRIAR whips off his robe revealing ROBIN HOOD.*)

ROBIN. Why don't you try me instead, Lord Sheriff!

SHERIFF. Robin Hood!
ROBIN. (*Drawing his sword.*) Right again!

(*The SHERIFF pushes ELLEN into ROBIN and draws his sword. The other two MONKS are revealed as LITTLE JOHN and FRIAR TUCK. RICCON and the FORESTERS draw swords as ALAN, MEG, and ARTHUR and whatever other MERRY MEN there are rush from the nearby woods. The PRIORESS heads for the castle door, but MARIAN heads her off, drawing a dagger. The PRIORESS does likewise. The action from here on must be carefully timed in such a way that the audience attention is not scattered, but focused on specific events. This may all be adapted according to the number of extras involved. A FORESTER jumps onto Tuck's back and is promptly thrown. Another FORESTER grabs him and TUCK hurls him into the wall. The KING draws his sword, is promptly met by ALAN-A-DALE and THEY fight. MEG grapples with the third FORESTER. The BISHOP cowers by the food table, eating nervously. HILTON sword-fights with ARTHUR. TUCK battles the first FORESTER he encountered. LITTLE JOHN goes after the BISHOP who throws food at him. RICCON clouts MEG from behind and SHE goes down. RICCON and the FORESTER are about to skewer her when LITTLE JOHN comes to her aid, parrying their swords with his quarterstaff. HILTON manages to hit ARTHUR with a stool and when ROBIN comes to his aid HE finds HE must contend with both HILTON and the SHERIFF. The PRIORESS has MARIAN up against the wall. SHE thrusts her dagger. MARIAN moves aside and it hits the wall. MARIAN slashes, wounding the PRIORESS*

*in the arm, disarming her. RICCON and the FORESTER
still battle LITTLE JOHN.)*

RICCON. I'll take him! Get Robin Hood!

*(The FORESTER hops up on the terrace to join the SHERIFF
and HILTON in cornering the furiously battling ROBIN
HOOD who leaps onto the table, parrying all three. TUCK
stabs the FORESTER he's been fighting, makes the sign
of the cross and goes after the BISHOP. The FORESTER
who TUCK threw into the wall recovers and fights with
ARTHUR. ALAN disarms the SHERIFF. LITTLE JOHN
gets the better of RICCON and clouts him soundly with
his staff. ELLEN hits HILTON with a serving tray and
ROBIN wounds the FORESTER leaving him alone with
the SHERIFF. MEG and ARTHUR subdue the last
FORESTER and all now focus on the final grand duel;
ROBIN vs. the SHERIFF. This may take in any and all of
the playing area, up and down the ramp, on tables and
chairs, across the terrace wall.)*

SHERIFF. It was meant to come down to this, Robin
Hood! The best with the best!
ROBIN. You flatter yourself, My Lord!
SHERIFF. That's the spirit! Already I sense a greater
opponent than Master Will Gamwell!
ROBIN. But less of a man, it was, that beat him!
SHERIFF. Clearly the fellow was out of his league!
ROBIN. If it's *your* league you mean, he'd be grateful for
that!
SHERIFF. Then you too must be grateful—! *(HE deftly
disarms Robin.)* ... since you are also exempt ...

*(ALL watch tensely as HE backs ROBIN HOOD up. The SHERIFF slashes and ROBIN leaps over it, turns and twists the sword from the SHERIFF'S grasp. THE SHERIFF leaps up onto the terrace, grabbing a sword from a fallen FORESTER. ROBIN with the Sheriff's sword, rushes up the ramp and THEY clash. At the top of the ramp the SHERIFF raises for a massive blow. ROBIN thrusts. The SHERIFF cries out, freezes, and then tumbles down the ramp to the bottom. Cheers go up from the VICTORS. MARIAN runs to embrace Robin. At sword point, the KING and BISHOP are lead to the center of proceedings by TUCK and LITTLE JOHN. The PRIORESS and the others are restrained by the rest of the BAND. ELEANOR continues to watch, as SHE has, from the side.)*

LITTLE JOHN. His Majesty King John!

ROBIN. Well, well! What's it to be then?! A double beheading?! A double draw-and-quarter ... *(Under his breath.)* Let's see, that would be dividing into eighths, that would make it—How many parts?

KING. You wouldn't dare!

BISHOP. Don't *dare* him! That's *all* they'd need! A challenge!

KING. Mother—Mother dear ... Talk some sense to them, won't you?

ELEANOR. You're right, John, I should. *(Pause while SHE walks to Robin.)* Draw-and-quarter is really too involved. Why don't you just behead them.

BISHOP. *(Panicking.)* That's talking sense?! Don't ask *her* for any more help—Please!

KING. Robin Hood, I grant you full pardon! You and all your men!

ROBIN. What do you say to that?

LITTLE JOHN. Then we can live like others.

TUCK. No more outlaws.

ALAN. No one to keep an eye on the likes of them.

MARIAN. No one to balance the books and see to the poor.

ROBIN. Well, that doesn't sound good at all. Your Majesty ... I just don't think we're worthy of pardons.

*(ROBIN motions to some jugs of wine which MEG and ARTHUR fetch. TUCK and LITTLE JOHN, wielding swords, bend the KING and BISHOP's heads down. The BISHOP shrieks.)*

KING. Wait! See here! There must be some agreement we can make!

ROBIN. Cut taxes by three quarters.

KING. Never.

BISHOP. *Never*—!!

KING. That would be absurd.

BISHOP. Be absurd! For God sakes, be absurd!

*(The swords are raised.)*

KING. All right! All right! Three quarters it is!

ROBIN. Hup! Too late!

*(ROBIN gives the sign. TUCK and LITTLE JOHN chop their swords heavily into the ground as MEG and ARTHUR*

*pour the wine over the necks of the screaming KING and*
*BISHOP.)*

BISHOP. Oh good lord! Good lord, I'm still alive! I'm still
alive! That must mean my head is still alive! I'm just a head!
I've heard of this happening! Like a chicken! Oh God, the
embarrassment!

KING. Hereford ...

BISHOP. (*Screaming.*) Your head's alive too!

KING. Hereford, shut up. We're not dead.

BISHOP. No! But we're just heads! Living heads! Gabbling
on! Talking in the dirt for all eternity! It's our punishment!

KING. The Sheriff was right. You *are* a ninny.

ROBIN. Three quarters it is then!  Tuck, show him the
place to sign!

*(TUCK draws out a parchment. The KING signs it on LITTLE*
*JOHN's back while the BISHOP examines his neck and*
*shoulders.)*

ELEANOR. I'll see that my goodly stout-hearted son keeps
his word.

ROBIN. Much thanks, Your Majesty. Now, since we're so
hungry and thirsty after all that fighting, I suggest we make
use of Nottingham Castle for a little while.

*(ROBIN's BAND cheer and rush through the door. The last*
*two, TUCK and LITTLE JOHN, struggle to go in first.*
*ROBIN and MARIAN wait for them and decide to kill the*
*time with a kiss. TUCK sees this and nudges LITTLE*
*JOHN with a smile. LITTLE JOHN turns to watch them,*

*smiling, and TUCK immediately rushes in. LITTLE JOHN
hastens after him.)*

KING. What a lovely couple ... Mother, if I paid for the
wedding ... would you let me conquer France?

*(MUSICIANS strike up. LIGHTS FADE.)*

## END OF PLAY

## PRODUCING ROBIN HOOD

Robin Hood is a big play. But it should *not* be an intimidating one. When first produced it was performed outside. The trees were real and the castle scenes were performed on a raised dirt stage, with a wooden ramp, banners, torches and backdrop. Simple.

And it can be just as simple indoors, with a little ingenuity and a little imagination. And a little budget. If you have a big budget, knock yourself out. If not—here are a few suggestions.

Divide your playing space in half. On stage right use a painted flat or backdrop to represent the Sheriff's castle. In front of this mount some platforms and surround them with a short wall. This is the Sheriff's terrace, where most of the castle's action takes place. It need not be high up—a few feet is fine. It might be one level or a few, depending on your needs and number of platforms. The entrance to the castle proper can be offstage in the case of a backdrop, or, in the case of a flat, right through a constructed onstage doorway. Embellish the terrace with torches and tapestries, and there you have it.

Place a small artificial garden at the foot of this terrace and you have the simple setting for the two London scenes between King John and Eleanor. Alter the lighting slightly to take the focus off the terrace. The audience will get it. People are only too happy to use their imagination, with a little help.

For the climactic wedding and battle royal, place a ramp descending from the terrace to stage level. That and the long table should provide for much hopping and swashbuckling. So much for the civilized half of the stage.

Stage left will take care of all forest needs. Now you don't need a hundred trees. A painted backdrop can suggest the depth and density of the woods, while a few well placed trees in front, including one large central one, will provide both cover for the actors and dimension. These can perhaps be built into a platform, or constructed each with its own base. Two dimensional trees will look three dimensional from the audience.

Adjust the lights to vary the look; darker, more ominous for Tanner's Grove and the Much and Guy scenes—brighter, cheerier, more expansive for Greenwood Glen and the Bishop's arrival.

For the Robin/Little John meeting simply use a piece suggesting a toppled log (either mobile or permanent). Stage level is fine for this. No height is necessary. Even if it looks like both men could easily pass, that's not what the scene is about. Look who we're dealing with here.

The Blue Boar Inn is easy enough. As the script states; keg, table, benches, barrel and board moved right in front of Sherwood.

As for costumes, a mixture of medieval and Elizabethan is fine—pull things from stock if you have it. Be inventive—this is "never never" history.

I do suggest that a combat coach assist with the fighting. Fights should be run before every performance. He or she might also give you a lead on sword rental. For much of what I have discussed, keep in mind BAKER'S PLAYS offers a fine technical library. Tell them what you need.

There are three traditional songs used in the play. There are probably numerous sources for this music, but I will list the ones I know. "Metaphysical Tobacco" is featured on *The Riverside Treasury of Music*, Houghton Mifflin Co., London Records Special Projects (2 CSL 1003). "Spotted Cow" is on Steeleye Span's *Below the Salt* Album, Chrystalis Records

(CHR 1008). And "The Treadmill Song" is also on a Steeleye Span, *Storm Force Ten* (CHR 1151). If you cannot find these, be creative. These songs have been handed down for a long time, and they'll survive a new interpretation, I'm sure.

On British accents; The script calls for a wide range, from the "veddy veddy" overdone upper crust of the Bishop; to King John's quiet refinement; Eleanor, Marian and the Prioress' more casual dialect; the Sheriff's ringing sharpness and clarity; the slightly countrified middle range of Robin, Will, Little John, Tuck, and Guy, to the rougher even cockney tones of Alan, Arthur, Meg and the Foresters. Much and Ellen could fit either of the latter.

Finally, the pacing. I can think of no play more suited to a brisk pace from stem to stern. The wordplay will fly and work best this way. Above all have fun. So will your audience.

# THE PRINCE WHO WOULDN'T TALK

## *A Comedy for Children*
### *and*
## *A Lesson for Adults*

### by JAMES BROCK

### Flexible Casting of 2 Men, 6 Women

Bare Stage with Pieces—55 Minutes

The King and Queen discover that their son, the Prince, doesn't talk. The pretty young Maiden points out this fact, but they do not listen to her either. Consequently, the royal couple put the Prince through a series of probing tests conducted by their zany three wizards. Of course, there is nothing wrong with the Prince but by now he has lost his confidence and is afraid to speak. When it looks like every effort to get him to talk is going to fail, the young Maiden discovers a way: she announces that she is going to leave the kingdom forever. In order to stop her, the Prince must speak out, which he does, and all ends well.

A delightful children's theatre script which manages to be amusing, sensitive and thought provoking.

# NOODLE DOODLE BOX

### by PAUL MAAR
### Translated by ANITA and ALEX PAGE
### 3 Men or 3 Women or Mixed Cast
### Bare Stage with Pieces

Highly acclaimed throughout Europe, a television special and the most popular children's play in West Germany, *Noodle Doodle Box* is now available in the United States and Canada. This easy to tour assembly length p,ay offers a genuine experience in learning to share and to live together. Pepper and Zacharias, two delightful, clownish wags, possess a box/house/space—a private space which they refuse to share with one another. The r boxes are unique and each quite interesting in its own peculiar way. Suddenly an overbearing, pompous Drum Major appears, takes a liking to the boxes and uses Pepper's and Zacharias' competitive nature to pit them against one another in order to steal their boxes. The two louts realize that because they did not stand together as friends, the Drum Major was able to divide them. However, magically they get one new box which they learn to share and enjoy together. This highly important children's theatre piece is enormously funny, richly rewarding and a pleasure to play.

# ROBINSON AND FRIDAY

### by HANSJORG SCHNEIDER
### Translated by KENNETH and BARBL RUGG
### Adapted and Edited by CAROL KORTY
### 3 Men, 1 Woman—Larger Cast Possible
### Exterior

This delightful play is a gentle spoof on authority that speaks to children of all ages. It is the story of the shipwrecked Robinson who lives alone on a deserted island talking to a wooden puppet, Robby, and trying to deal with a pesty Gulala bird, while observing the strictest discipline in daily life. There can be no dancing ("it interferes with marching"), no singing and music ("it interferes with working"), until Friday happens on the scene. Robinson begins to teach the free-spirited Friday *his* way of life, but ultimately, it is Friday who is the teacher. Schneider's adaptation of the Defoe novel examines what we do to survive physically, what we must do to live with our inner selves, how we deal with our longings and fears and what adjustments we must make to live with others. "Tailor-made for giving youngsters an appreciation for theatre."—*Boston Globe.* "Lovely, beautiful and very funny. Something special and new."—*The Village Voice.*

# WITHOUT BATHROBES:

## *ALTERNATIVES IN DRAMA FOR YOUTH*

### by JACK KURTZ

#### *Three one-act plays for production by young people in churches and schools*

**THE HOLIDAY.** Satirical fantasy. 6 men, 8 women—flexible. Bare stage. Good King Teo's habit of propounding new rules on his birthday becomes intolerable, and he is given severance pay and sent packing by his subjects. Shortly after his departure there is the birth of a child, surrounded by mysterious circumstances. In need of a holiday to break the monotony, the people begin to celebrate Baby's Birthday. But Baby grows up and proves too threatening for the people's comfort—he is disposed of, although his birth continues to be celebrated. A stimulating look at what has happened to the meaning of Christmas. **THE COMPLAINT BOOTH.** Satirical farce. 20-40 persons—flexible. Bare stage. The World Chamber of Commerce decrees that Christmas will be celebrated 365 days a year "for philanthropic reasons." Finding that some souls are still not happy, the Chamber sets up a complaint department, complete with the amazing Sub-Atomic Quasi—Robotic Christmas Wish Good Fairies, who achieve some unexpected, and not quite satisfactory, results. An imaginative plea for putting Christ back in Christmas, backed with some none-too-gentle swipes at our ideas of happiness. **THE RETURN OF THE UNICORN.** Satirical farce. 10 men, 10 women—flexible. Bare Stage. A girl discovers a unicorn that fills her with uncontrollable excitement and awe. She rushes to tell the world of the being, only to find the world too frightened, too rational and too self-centered for awe and wonder. The little girl is faced with the sad duty of telling the unicorn it doesn't exist. The beautifully woven modern fable forthrightly questions whether there is room in our world for reverence and wonder at the coming of God.